BLEEDING PANTHER

A Novel By
Jodi Clark

AUTHOR'S NOTE: This story is a work of fiction. Names, characters, places and incidents are a product of the author's imagination and any resemblance to actual persons, places or events are entirely coincidental.

United States Copyright © 2015 Jodi Clark Published by Lulu

ISBN 978-0-9891207-5-3

A Special Thank You

This novel is dedicated to all of the United States military service men and women, both overseas and at home, current and former, who have so unselfishly pledged their lives and freedom for the sake of our country.

Each is a hero, in his or her own rite, respectable and proud, who deserves the utmost allegiance for their unwavering dedication. It is they who risk their lives at war, protecting us and our country, and protecting other countries and their inhabitants as well.

Let us always remember to give the proper courtesy and respect to all who have and continue to serve on our behalf, for they are our future.

Author Biography

Jodi Clark was born and raised in the panhandle of West Virginia, where she is married with a son and stepdaughter. Her family and home in the valley are her pride.

Discovering her passion for writing at the age of twelve, during an essay assignment for school, she began to nourish her new hobby writing poetry and short stories.

In 2008, she published her first novel, *The Disappearance of Benny,* followed by her second fiction novel, *Aiding Revenge,* in 2010 and *Matriarca,* in 2011.

CHAPTER 1

The rock and roll guitar riffs of the eighties blared from the stereo speakers, echoing throughout my modest but cozy home as I neared the end of my cleaning mission. It was always delightful to see the mid-day sun peeking through the windows onto spotless floors as the fresh aroma of pine filled the kitchen.

I rushed to the bathroom for a quick shower with the perfect new sundress and heels that I had laid out to wear. My long caramel locks would be gently swept up with only a few thin tresses draped down the nape of my bronzed neck, just the way that he liked it, and I dabbed myself with his favorite perfume. I aspired to look like the elegant, younger woman that he had married fifteen years before. My excitement had been brewing for days and it was about to boil over. Finally, after fourteen excruciating months, I would be able to wrap my arms around my husband again.

Adam had served in the Marines for about as long as we'd been married, enlisting at just twenty-one years old, and his years of dedication and sacrifice had promoted him to an officer of his unit. It was always his pleasure to serve his country and he was extremely proud to do it. He had dedicated himself wholeheartedly to the Marines and was prepared to give his life, at any time, for one of his "brothers" if necessary, just as any of them would have for him. As a military wife, his sacrifices were mine, as well, and I had elected to cope with being managed by the United States government. We abided by their decisions and we trusted them completely, even if we didn't always agree with their judgment. Where we lived, how we lived, how we spent our days were all decided by the military. It didn't always seem fair to me, but it was what I had married into and I accepted it without contention.

Adam's plane had finally carried him home from

the merciless bloodshed in Iraq, and I waited with the crowd of other anxious military wives and children to get a glimpse of our servicemen entering the room. American flags and signs, lovingly crafted by the hands of loved ones, crammed the crowd of onlookers in the enormous hangar, all in respectful anticipation of its military servant.

"When is daddy coming?" I heard a young girl ask, nearby.

"Soon, honey. Very soon," her fervent mother calmly replied, even though her trembling voice and constant pacing gave away her own enthusiasm.

My stomach ached with a blend of impatience and excitement until I felt I couldn't endure even another second of waiting. Already, I fought back the tears but they were joyful at the thought of holding the man I loved.

"Where is this damn plane?" I asked myself in impetuous silence, yearning to see my handsome husband walk toward me. Living independently, without our husbands, while keeping our daily routines with the children was more difficult than any woman who wasn't a military wife could comprehend. We didn't have the luxury of even speaking with them every day and always, there was the fear of never seeing them again. We could never know the full extent of what our loved ones were forced to endure overseas and, most of the time, they preferred not to talk about it anyway. My job was to be my husband's support system, and I always strove to be the best wife that I could be for him.

I recalled the news that I had gotten just a month prior, the knock on my front door that I had always dreaded. An officer of the military stood with his hat in his hands and concern on his face. I knew that something had happened to my husband. Reluctantly, I opened the door to what could have changed my life forever.

"Good afternoon, ma'am," he greeted somberly. "I'm sorry to disturb you, but may I have a few minutes of your time to speak with you about your husband?" I could feel the panic rushing through me.

"Of course." I invited the somber-faced, uniformed man inside to talk.

"Mrs. Koehley, I'm sorry to inform you that Adam has been captured by members of a terrorist cell in Iraq."

My breath escaped me and time stood still. I saw nothing, I heard nothing. Pure immense panic had taken over my body.

"We know that he's alive and believe that he's okay but just being held with some other people, and I'm here to assure you, Mrs. Koehley, that the United States Military is doing everything in its power to free them so try not to worry," he said.

"Try not to worry?" I thought. "What kind of wife could do that?" I was overcome with it, wondering what it was that they wanted from Adam and how afraid he must have been.

I prayed. I prayed harder than I ever had in my entire life, pleading with God to set my husband free. If they were like what I had always seen on the news, Adam could likely be beheaded. I couldn't stand the thought of it, and I didn't know how I could ever live without him. This man, who was always so courageous and kind, surely God wouldn't let him die that way, I thought. Each day that passed without a word was worse than the one before.

"No news is good news," I kept trying to reassure myself. Each day that they didn't come to my door meant that Adam was surviving. I knew how brave and level-headed he was. If anyone could cope, it was him.

Somehow, I still drifted through my days, taking care of our kids and keeping up with what needed to be done, living like a robot who was just going through the motions. It was the nights, alone in our bed, when I cried for him, yearned for him, pleaded for his life. There had always been a risk of him not coming home after a tour of duty. We lived with that every day but never really doubted his survival. This turn of events made it a real possibility that I would never see my husband alive again and that my kids would lose their father. The thought of his death suffocated me. I needed Adam like I needed air. In the privacy of my bedroom, I fell to my knees, wailing and pleading with God to bring him home safely. Four agonizing weeks later, he answered my prayers.

After what felt like an eternity to me, the massive airplane roared down the runway and the uniformed Marines began to appear, one by one at first, then growing in numbers. I watched with an eagle's eye as each soldier's family ran to their loved ones, leaping tearfully into their arms.

"Where is Adam?" I wondered, nervously, praying to God that he would show himself soon. Soldier after elated soldier drifted through the crowd to be joyfully reunited with their families, and I swore that if I didn't see him soon, I would leap onto that plane to find him.

Finally he appeared, the princely man in uniform, his dark hair closely shaven, looking even more handsome than I remembered. He walked with an honorable regard that I always admired. His eyes scanned the hoard for me while I selfishly pushed through to get to him.

"Adam!" I blurted and saw the grin of his strong jaw that had always melted me.

"Allison!" He rushed toward me just as fast as I ran to him, clenching each other as tightly as we could as I was lifted from the ground in his arms. After more than a year apart and almost losing him, I couldn't believe that I was holding him again. It didn't seem real. I relished the feel of him cradling me in his arms and the familiar scent of his skin in the fatigues that he wore. His lips were like satin on mine, and his soft kiss ignited the flame inside of me, just the way it had the very first time.

"You are so beautiful, babe. I missed you so much."

"I'm so happy you're home," I said, never wanting to let him go again. His arms were my haven.

His face still held the wounds from his captors, healing cuts and bruises that he'd been forced to endure in their custody. I had never been told by the military what had happened to him other than that he'd been rescued from them a week before he returned home, and it was classified information that I wasn't permitted to know. I realized how difficult it would be for me not to question him about what he went through, not to know what had happened to him there.

"It's nice to be back home with my amazing wife," he replied with a gracious smile. "How are the kids?"

"They can't wait to see you. I barely got them to sleep last night. I couldn't sleep either."

"Well, we've got a little time before school lets out so…" he spoke flirtatiously. It had been fourteen long months, after all.

"Let's go!" We giggled, promenading out of the hangar.

We lived on the military base at Kane'ohe Bay in Hawaii, in a modest, three bedroom house. It certainly wasn't spectacular, but it was always tidy and full of love. We felt blessed to be stationed in such a stunning place, surrounded by magnificently sculpted mountains, sunshine and the alluring aqua sea. It was a tourist's paradise, and it was ours, as well. We had been there for nearly ten years and had made bountiful memories together.

In our bedroom, my husband stared into my eyes with my face in his hands and a story of yearning. His vibrant blue eyes reeled me into his very soul until I nearly cried. Never could I remember wanting his touch the way that I did at that moment.

"I missed you so much," he whispered with damp eyes and began kissing me passionately, hungrily claiming my lips as we undressed each other. His flesh against mine seemed to reconnect our souls, rekindling the wildly burning flame that fueled our marriage, our love pouring out to each other into eruptions of erotic ecstasy.

"Wow! That was incredible," Adam complimented after we made love and I agreed, breathless and jovial. His caress had nourished me. My heart fluttered with the excitement of new love, the same as it had when we had first met.

"I missed you so much, babe," I told him. "I'm so glad you're home." He held me in the strength of his arms snugly against him.

"This feels so good, holding you like this. I thought of you every single day. I just can't imagine life without you. Knowing you were here is what got me through."

"I'm so happy you're home and safe," I told him. "I love you so much."

"I love you, too, sweetheart, more than anything."

We arrived at the elementary school, situated not far from our house on base, a half hour early for Adam to surprise Anabel and Andrew.

"May I go to their classes?" He kindly asked the principal and, with his permission, we entered Anabel's second grade classroom, decorated in vividly colored drawings that the children had made and pictures of animals and numbers. "Where's my beautiful Anabel?"

"Daddy!" Our petite, sandy-haired daughter ran over and jumped, joyfully, into Adam's arms.

"Hi, baby girl," he greeted, squeezing her tightly with moist eyes and a smile. "Daddy missed you so much." Her teacher and I, both, shared in the tears as her classmates cheered.

"Koeley, front and center!" Adam playfully shouted in Andrew's fifth grade class. Our son lifted his head with timid eyes to find that it was the voice of his father. His courageous attempt to fight back tears failed as he proudly approached Adam with a hug. "I've missed you, son," his dad greeted. "Have you upheld your duty as the man of the house while I was away?"

"Yes, sir," Andrew respectfully answered, like a soldier. His father had always been his hero and he tailored himself after him, imitating Adam's character and personality, often even dressing like him. Andrew's aspiration was to follow in his father's footsteps as a dedicated Marine. He played the part flawlessly, assuming the role of his father in his absence, maintaining strength and courage for the family. He was our protector and the man of the house while his father was gone. Andrew took over the tasks of his father, things like mowing the lawn and taking out the trash, not because he was asked to but because he wanted to. He carried himself as a young Marine, a soldier in his own rite and on his own mission. He was his father's son and I was extremely proud.

I could almost see the relief in my son when he saw his mentor, like the weight had been shifted back to his father's shoulders and he could finally be a child again, even if just for a little while. Adam's tours overseas had forced Andrew to grow up faster than he needed to, much like many other boys his age.

"Let's celebrate with some ice cream," my husband suggested to the kids in the car, and they cheered with delight.

"Honey, they haven't had dinner yet," I tried to argue, but it was to no avail.

As we sat together as a family, I thought about how grateful I was for us all to be together again, and I thanked God for it. Adam had served several lengthy tours overseas and each time he was forced to leave, our children suffered, deprived of their father in his absence and sorely aware that he may never return. Even though they understood that it was the life of a military family, it never got easier, and they would never grow accustomed to it. The void had, once again, been filled. Adam's return was our reward for the sacrifices that we made, but it was never guaranteed. Looming over our heads was the possibility of his demise on any given mission. Every military family's worst fear was a visit from officers. I was thankful that we hadn't been forced to endure such a loss, the way that other families we knew had and, as I watched my children savoring the presence of their father, my smile couldn't be broken.

That night, Adam and I made love again, and I cherished the feel of him, the scent of his warm, soft skin and hair, the contour of his refined arms, the sound of his breath. As I lay, peacefully coddled in his embrace, I wished we could stay that way forever.

"I love you so much," I whispered to him in the dim silence.

"I love you even more, baby doll," he softly responded. "It's so nice to be back in bed with you."

A few hours later, I was jolted awake by the shrill screams of my husband that echoed from the dining room. It was the shriek of terror that I had only heard in horror movies, and it catapulted me into a panic. Adam was fighting with an intruder, I thought and, terrified to leave our bedroom, I knew that I had to protect him and our children. I grabbed the lamp from my nightstand and forced my trembling body down the dark hallway as his screams grew more prevalent. Peering cautiously through the obscured living room from the end of the hallway revealed nothing, and I continued on my path toward Adam, petrified of what I might see. His screams were the only sounds in the night, and I feared what was happening. His screams led me through the blackness, and I turned on the light to see my husband crouched under the dining room table, trembling and sweating. He glared at me with amplified eyes of apprehension and nervousness.

"Get back!" He yelled at me with his hands formed to his imaginary weapon. "Stay back!"

I was plagued with angst because I had never before

experienced what was happening. Adam seemed to have transported himself back to the war in his mind, and I knew that he saw me as the predator rather than his wife. He was trained to kill and capable of anything, especially when he felt threatened, the way he did at that moment. I was frozen in place like a child before a vicious dog, afraid of provoking him.

"Honey, it's me, Allison," I softly reminded, but he appeared unfazed. His mind was still on the battlefield. "It's Allison, honey, your wife," I repeated in an attempt to rescue him from his nightmare but only from where I stood.

"You're not taking me!" He shouted. "Please! Please don't!" Sweat streamed from his ashen skin as he cowered in a ball within his shelter, shivering with the horror from the visions in his mind.

"What do I do?" I wondered, battling my panic. I knew not to move any closer to him, and I prayed that the kids didn't come rushing out and startle him. I was surprised but relieved that they hadn't woken up to the ruckus, and I was doing my best to calm the situation.

"I love you," I asserted in a desperate plea, my voice shaky and fearful. "Adam, I love you. You're home. You're okay now." His fearful stare into my eyes was unwavering for what seemed like forever. "You're home and you're safe, honey. I love you." Finally, my words began to release him from his trance, and his glare softened to confusion while he assessed the situation.

"What's going on?" He inquired, as if he didn't recall the episode. Humiliation accompanied him from underneath the rectangular wooden table as wiped the sweat from his face and crawled out, wondering why he was there in the first place.

"Sit down, honey, and I'll make you some hot tea," I told my baffled husband. I recognized his shame and wanted to console him.

"No thanks, babe. I'm okay," he replied with a soft

tone that was almost apologetic. I could see him working through his confusion.

"Are you sure?"

"Yeah," he assured. "Let's go back to bed." He lay in my arms as I quietly caressed his forehead. "That's nice," he commented softly, drifting back to sleep.

I didn't know what, in particular, had triggered the flashback but I could only assume that it was from his capture. Adam had experienced horrific things in Iraq that I knew would probably live with him for the rest of his days. There were things that he had likely seen that I would never even know about, things that he would bury deep inside. My heart ached for him and what he had been through there. I wasn't sure there was a man there that could return home without some lasting effects from the war.

CHAPTER 2

I wanted Adam to talk about what had happened to him in Iraq, what he had been through there. He had never really been one to particularize his experiences during his tours of duty, always very vague when I inquired about them, and it was blaringly obvious that even bringing the subject up made him uncomfortable. I often wondered if his silence was to protect me or to protect him.

"War is everything you'd expect it to be," he had spoken of Iraq. "The sun was oppressive and the nights were muggy. We ate and slept when there was an opportunity, and we always watched our backs. Once in a while, I would get lucky enough to sleep in a tent or rooftop but, most of the time, I slept in the dirt with my backpack or jacket as a pillow or propped up against one of the Jeeps. There were times that I would have given anything for just a patch of grass to lie on, you know? Everything there is dirt and concrete. There's no color." As an officer, he didn't have to endure those sleeping conditions, but he chose to because of his brothers, he had mentioned. "If they were going to suffer, then I was, too." Adam's unit was there to offer protection to the villages in the more volatile cities. They patrolled the towns, hunting down government targets while keeping the villagers protected while providing them with food and other essentials. Adam talked about how he had done everything from battling Iraqi rebels to just playing ball with some of the children. His comrades had dubbed him the panther for his sneak attacks on the enemy, and a part of him welcomed the challenge to play his part in protecting others. He didn't want to be the guy overseeing what his unit did. He wasn't happy unless he was in the thick of it with them and, because of that, they all had great respect for him. Still, I knew that there were parts of it that he was intentionally leaving out, especially regarding his capture. He wasn't the same man who had left our home for Iraq.

The morning evoked my usual ritual of getting the kids fed and off to school as the soothing sun peeked out on the morning dew. It promised a day of new possibilities. I sat, sipping my steaming coffee on the back deck that looked out at the sea as the sun warmed my arms. The songs of the seagulls captured the silence of the tropical air as the sun's reflection danced in the gentle ripples. With my eyes closed, I breathed in the fresh morning, appreciative of its offering. It was always the best part of my day, almost therapeutic.

My mind travelled back to Adam's episode during the night, but I wished that I could just let it go. It still held steadfast in my head since I had never experienced it before, and I wondered if he'd had them while he was away. I worried about him and about our children seeing their father that way. Most of all, I wondered how to handle any future episodes, especially if they grew worse, and how to get him help for them.

Adam had a couple of days off before he had to return to work on base, and I wanted to make the best of them, so I began with breakfast in bed.

"Whoa, what's all this?" He asked with a gracious smile when I presented the tray of fluffy, buttered pancakes and sausage links to him. I nestled under the covers beside of him. "You even warmed the syrup?"

"I just wanted you to know how happy I am to have you home," I told him. "You deserve it after all you've been through."

"Wow, this is so great, babe," he said as he savored his first home cooked breakfast in months. "I'm happy to be home. It's true what they say – there's no place like it."

"Especially after that place," I replied of Iraq.

"This sure beats oatmeal in a tin cup every morning," he remarked. "After all of that sand and dirt, I never knew that I could appreciate the small things so much, like breakfast in bed, sleeping in and grass," he snickered. "It was so nice to sleep in our bed again, cuddled up next to you and holding you. It feels great."

"Yes, it does," I agreed. "Sleeping in our bed without you is never easy."

After breakfast, Adam and I made love, playfully and passionately, like newlyweds who couldn't get enough of each other. Never had I loved anyone the way that I loved him, and I wanted him to know it. We always treasured the time that we had together, aware that another deployment could halt it any time. It kept our relationship strong, and we appreciated the love we had for each other even more. We had learned not to take each other for granted. He and I had the kind of marriage that everyone wished for, and we were truly in love.

The two of us spent our entire morning in bed together, watching television and talking, without anywhere else to be. The day was ours, alone, and its freedom felt wonderful. I wished every day could be the same. As much as I wanted to talk about what had happened with him during the night, I didn't want to inflict any more embarrassment on him or ruin our joyful moments together. I knew that he would talk to me about it when he was comfortable.

"Let's go outside," I suggested, gleefully.

"Or we could just stay in bed longer," Adam responded flirtatiously.

"Babe!" I giggled. "Let's get some fresh air."

The brilliant sun warmed the day under clear blue skies, a paradise of our very own outside. The joyful hymns of the birds greeted us as we sat on the back porch.

"It's so nice here," Adam remarked with a deep breath of euphoria and I stared with concurrence, "so colorful. This is the good side of the military."

"Take your shoes off," I commanded, playfully. "What?"

"Just do it," I insisted. We stripped off our shoes and I led my husband into the freshly mowed grass. "How does that feel?"

"Ah, it's amazing," he grinned. "Feels like home."

"I have a surprise for you." He followed me to a blanket spread on the lawn that held a picnic basket and freshly-picked, tropical flowers that I had snuck out of bed and quickly set up while he showered.

"What's all this?" He appeared impressed by my efforts. "You're spoiling me, baby girl." We sat in the shade, enjoying the light lunch of sandwiches and fruit that I had prepared. "Wine, too?" Adam added with surprise. "I could really get used to this."

"I know it's only noon but it is a celebration, after all, of you being back home with us."

"Wow, sweetheart, this is great, and it sure beats Iraq," he said. "I'm such a lucky man."

"I'm the lucky one," I insisted and raised my glass for a toast. "To an extended stay."

"And an amazing wife," he added.

Alone with only good conversation and the sounds of the ocean, I relished my husband's presence. I was thrilled to have him back home and wanted to make it enjoyable for him. I wanted him to see how much I truly did appreciate him. With his aqua eyes staring into mine and my hands in his, I fell in love all over again.

"How did I get so lucky," he complimented, raising his hand to my cheek, "to have such a beautiful and wonderful wife?" His words converted me into a blushing school girl. "I love you so much, Allison. You and this family truly are my everything."

"And you are ours," I responded, returning his trance. "I'm so proud of who you are, and I never want to live without you. I don't know how I could."

"As long as God grants me breath, you'll never have to. You're my heartbeat, my soul, and there's nothing I won't do for you. I just want to spend all the rest of my days with you and our children."

"We will always love and support you, no matter what," I replied with saturated eyes. "There's nothing in the world that I won't do for you."

Living our military life wasn't always easy. Most of the time, I felt like a single mother because he wasn't able to be home with us, but I felt so blessed to have such a wonderful man as my husband, and I was certain that there couldn't be a better one in the world. I adored Adam and respected him for the remarkable person that he was. There was nothing that he wouldn't do for another. He had even earned a medal of honor for saving his fellow soldiers on the line of duty. Adam was an admirable man who was respected by his peers, someone who would offer his last bite of food to another, even if he was starving. He believed in helping those around him and treating everyone kindly, and he'd been that way his entire life. Everyone who knew Adam loved him.

"I have one more surprise for my favorite Marine," I told him. "I booked you a fishing trip for the day." Deep sea fishing had always been one of Adam's favorite pastimes, though he didn't get to do it as much as he liked. I couldn't think of a better way to spend his first full day back.

"Babe, you're so amazing. That's awesome!"

"So you'd better get down to the marina and catch that boat."

"Where's Dad?" Andrew asked when I got him and his sister home from school.

"I sent him on a fishing trip for the day, but he'll be back in a couple hours. Now, how about helping me out with dinner?"

"We're not having fish again, are we?" He inquired. "No, no fish tonight," I vowed with a chuckle.

"I'm glad Daddy's back home," Anabel said. "I

hope he stays here forever."

"Me too, baby girl," I replied.

"Will he have to go back to Iraq?" Andrew asked but I didn't have the answer.

"I don't know, buddy," I said. "I guess that depends on the military, but I sure hope that it's a long while before he does. You know how important his job is. People need him and depend on him, just like we do. He has to sacrifice some of his time with us to help them, right?"

"I know," he said.

"Dad doesn't like being away from us, but he has made a commitment to the government. We always miss him, but we can't allow ourselves to be selfish with him, right?"

"Yes," he answered.

"Besides, that's what has taught you to be such a good man, which I'm very grateful for. I'm so proud of you and your sister. You guys are my world and I love you very much."

"I love you, too, Mom," he replied.

Adam pulled into the driveway just in time for dinner.

"How was it?" I inquired.

"Oh, babe, it was so awesome! I caught some big guys and have already cleaned and filleted them. They're in the freezer in the garage. What a great day. I'm taking you with me next time, bud," he told Andrew.

"When can I go, too?" Our daughter intervened.

"Whenever you want, sweetness," Adam replied. "Can you clean a fish?"

"Give it a bath?" She said and we erupted in laughter.

"Well, something like that," her father responded. "We have to cut off the head. Can you do that?" She curled up her nose with disgust at the thought of it.

"I'll probably just stay home with Mommy," she

replied softly in a quick change of heart.

That evening, after dinner, I watched from the kitchen as Adam sat with the kids, playing board games. Their laughter brought out my best smile and I thanked God, once again, for the blessing. I never wanted to know life without my family. They were my everything.

"You should've seen the marlin I reeled in, babe," Adam gloated.

"Big ones, huh?"

"Enormous! I filled up the freezer out there," he exclaimed. "Thanks so much for the trip. I really needed that after so much time in the dirt."

"Speaking of that," I began hesitantly, "I just want to make sure you're okay after what happened last night." I tiptoed around the subject as delicately as I could, already aware that he wouldn't want to talk about the episode.

"Yeah, babe, I'm okay," he responded casually. "It's all okay."

"Was it from your capture over there?" I probed. "I mean, I know you've been through a lot."

"It was just a nightmare, babe," he replied with a hint of agitation and I wasn't willing to ruin our night together by pushing the issue.

CHAPTER 3

The late night brought a tumultuous echo of the one before with Adam's jolting shrieks piercing the silent darkness.

"Stop! Get back!" He yelped from our bed before rolling out of it. Unlike the previous night, he'd only made it as far as the vanity, on the far side of our bedroom, where he cowered as a fearful child beneath it. The maple desk lent itself his cramped haven in my husband's torturous nightmare. "Get back!" He warned as I approached. He had a tight grasp on my hairbrush, which tried to force a giggle out of me, but I couldn't make light of a serious situation. I found that the fear wasn't as great as the night before, and I felt confident that I could bring Adam back to reality again.

"It's me, honey," I softly spoke, "Allison." The previous night's tactic was certain to work again, I thought.

"No!" He screamed and bolted into our bathtub.

"Babe, it's okay. It's your wife and I love you."

I took a small step toward him and, for the first time ever in our relationship of more than fifteen years, my mellow and doting husband dropped the brush and lunged at me, the enemy in his unconscious world. His brawny hands clenched my tender throat with intent to kill as he threw me down on the floor. Unable to speak from the overwhelming pressure, I began to punch his arms and head, desperate to wake him from our battle, but my defense only provoked him to increase his strength. My eyes bulged with terror as I struggled for my waning breath, punching and kicking, slipping in and out of consciousness, and I knew that if I let my body go limp, I would die. As long as my body could struggle, I was still alive, but I knew I couldn't survive his strength for much longer. It could have only been God who brought our young daughter to our bedroom, knocking on the door. The interruption startled

Adam out of his trance and, all of the sudden, I felt his hands release and air gushing into my esophagus as I hacked continuously to recover. Her knocking had frightened him as she walked in.

"I heard a noise," she spoke, sleepily rubbing her eyes. My relentless coughing and gasping refused me a response to her concern as I continued to recover. "Are you alright, Mommy?" Anabel queried while patting me on the back. All I could think about was how to get her back to her bedroom before her father continued his escapade. I pointed toward the door to motion her back to her room just as Adam reappeared in our bedroom.

"Oh my God, babe, are you alright?" He probed, frantically attempting to aid me. "Are you alright? I'm so sorry, babe. I'm so sorry, sweetheart." Relief blessed me to hear his normal tone again.

"Daddy, I heard a noise."

"It's okay, sweetheart," he consoled, trying to keep her calm. "Go back to bed and Daddy will be there in just a few minutes. I'm going to get Mommy a drink of water."

I tried to stand up as my head reeled and my ears rang stridently. My eyes strained to focus while I continued to recoup my breath. Nausea set in, immediately, in an eerie feeling of being brought back to life.

"What happened?" Adam probed with concern. "What have I done?" He sat with me on the bed, his arm wrapped around me while he struggled to recall what had taken place. All he knew was that he'd found himself with his hands around my neck. "Oh, God, baby, I'm so sorry. I'm so sorry."

I was vacant of words, unable to muster even a single syllable, as if mute from the shock of it all. Maybe I should have felt anger or even fear, at that moment, for what my husband had done to me, but all I could feel was gratefulness that his attack on me had been interrupted. I was sure that my life had just been saved by our daughter.

"Sweetheart, I'm so sorry. I'm so sorry," he dropped down to his knees before me with my hands in his, and I could feel his repentance. I knew that my husband would never have done that in his right frame of mind.

Together we sobbed, uncontrollably, as he held me, and I thought about how ironic it was that the lethal arms that threatened my life were the same ones that consoled me. I couldn't fault him for his actions. It was just another scar that the war had left behind. His suffering was far worse than mine. Still, I found myself struggling to trust him. I was terrified of my own husband, fearful of the person that I had always trusted most in my life, this man who was trained to kill with his bare hands, yet I still yearned for his solace. Without a word, Adam and I nestled under the covers as he cradled me in his arms. It remained my place of security, where his embrace soothed me back to sleep.

The morning hadn't cured me of my anxiety as I got the kids up for breakfast. I tied a decorative scarf around my neck to hide the marks that had been left on me from the night before.

"Why were you coughing so much last night, Mommy?" My inquisitive daughter asked.

"You know, I'm not sure. I think I just had a frog in my throat."

"Frogs can't get in your throat," my son joined the conversation.

"If you swallow them, they can," his sister responded.

"Okay, enough of the frog talk," I interrupted. "We have to get you to school."

Inviting sunshine welcomed me onto the sun-heated boards of the deck under my feet. With my coffee, I stared out toward the aqua waters of the ocean, searching my soul for forgiveness of my husband, for a solution to his problem. Things weren't normal anymore, and I wondered if they ever would be again. For the first time ever, I feared the man who loved me most in the world, the person I trusted the most, and I didn't know how to get through it. This time, he owed me an explanation of what had happened in Iraq, I told myself.

"Good morning, sweetheart," Adam greeted, softly from behind, with his arms wrapped around me. The gentle kiss of his lips on my neck sent a flutter through my heart while causing me to cringe, all at the same time.

"Hi," I responded with my hands in his. Shame invaded his face when he removed the scarf and saw the bruises on my neck.

"I'm so sorry about last night," he apologized again. "Look what I've done. I feel like such a jerk and I didn't mean to…"

"I know you didn't," I interrupted. "I just wonder about the next time, or the time after that, you know? I mean, I've never been through this with you before this. You're a different person than when you left." He dropped his woeful eyes to the ground, overwhelmed with guilt for what he had done to his wife.

"I'm so sorry, babe," he repeated. "I feel like nothing can fix this, what I did to you. I'm just not myself when…"

"I know that it wasn't really you, Adam," I responded with a deep breath, "that it was a marine defending himself. How can I blame you for that?"

"But you don't trust me anymore now. I love you more than anything else in this world, Allison, and I would never hurt you intentionally. I would die before I hurt you, but look what I've done, your neck." Tears fell from his eyes. "I really hurt you, and the problem is that I couldn't control it. In my head, I was still over there."

"I know you didn't mean to," I replied with my hand on his cheek, his tears inviting mine. "We just have to get you the help that you need." He hung his head with indignity in his heart.

"I thought it would go away," he admitted in a tone of distress. I thought that I just needed to come home." Adam explained that his nightmares began after only a few weeks in Iraq. "It was different this time," he said, "different from any other tour. The atmosphere, the tension, the fear, it was all heightened there. I saw and experienced things that I can't even talk about yet."

"I know you did, sweetheart, and I know how hard it is for you to talk about, but you need to this time. I deserve to know what's going on." He nodded with a deep breath.

"It's a different world over there." Adam spoke of the Iraqi people in their small villages of unstable shelters, disease and starvation, everyone in fear and distrusting others. "The pain of looking into the eyes of those helpless kids, starving and fearful, and the parents who had no way to even help them just killed me inside. There's no freedom. They're at the mercy of so many evils." He spoke of the crippling torture that the villagers had endured and their fear of their country's leader and several terrorist groups. "It was even worse for us, as Americans, and especially military. Every single second was a gamble of our lives. We were being shot at and bombed by devils and, most of the time, we couldn't tell the good from the bad. They were like wolves in sheep's clothing, trying to fool us with mischievous smiles. Those people have no conscience and, worse, they do it in God's name. They shot at us from rooftops, buried bombs in the dirt, even trained the children to shoot at us – young children. We were forced to entrust complete strangers with our lives, people we never met until we got there." He described the brotherhood that had developed among the soldiers stationed there, who arrived as strangers but held their lives in one another's hands, and he communicated their vow to keep each other safe. "One would give his life for another, even if he didn't know him, and even if he didn't like him. In the civilian world, we might be dire enemies but, at war, we were brothers," he said. "I was responsible for them, and I couldn't send them into the lion's den while I stayed behind." His words flowed as if he had held them inside for a lifetime but yearned to free them, and they granted a sense of release to him as he spoke. It was clear to me that he needed to get his thoughts out, and I listened with silent respect as he expressed his sentiments. His compassion for the Iraqi citizens grasped my very soul, the way that he had made it his mission to protect them.

I found myself analyzing the words of his candid dialogue for what had so vividly altered the man I married. Of every sentence he communicated, none surrendered itself the answer. It was what I needed the most. I needed Adam to talk about his capture and what had happened during those three weeks so that I could, somehow, save my husband from his demons. Maybe I should have asked. I should have demanded to know what happened there, but his statements had stolen my courage. Perhaps Adam still just couldn't talk about it. Maybe it was too soon, I thought, but I couldn't go on each night fearing the monster who stalked me. I had left the conversation a wimp, too meek and afraid to say what I knew that I should have.

I went about my day, as if any other, dutifully following my schedule of errands, housework and dinner as Adam worked in the yard. From the window, I observed him performing the work that needed to be done, without complaint and without argument. It was his life, following orders the way that a marine is trained to do. He was almost robotic in his responsibilities, performing the job at hand with flawless precision. I admired him for his discipline and I respected him for his honor, but my anger was overpowering as I watched. I began to dub my husband selfish and inconsiderate for his lack of explanation, his lack of compassion for my demand of answers. He had deprived me of the vindication that I needed. Adam hadn't taken any steps to try and correct the problem, and I couldn't get past the disappointment I felt because of it. I needed something from him, a show of effort, I suppose. I feared the fighter in him, and I needed him to sympathize with me. Then, my guilt intervened.

"How could I be so self-absorbed?" I asked myself. Adam had been through more agony than I could even fathom and, there I was, in my own game of self-pity. It was I who was being selfish. Suddenly, I felt terrible for my ill feelings toward my husband, and I regretted them. Adam was an honorable man struggling with the effects of war. It didn't make him anything less than the hero he'd always been, and I felt ashamed for weakening his character.

That night, he went to bed early, and I debated my sleeping arrangements. I yearned to rest in the arms of the man I loved but my fear battled it. Still, the risk outweighed the reward and I snuggled next to him in bed, praying for a peaceful night.

Three hours later, I awoke in darkness and the sound of my husband's soft snores. Relief engulfed me to see him finally getting a good night's rest, and I prayed it stayed that way. My bladder tried to persuade me into a trip to the bathroom but my fear of rattling Adam debated it. I was afraid to make any movements as I lay still on my back, but the more I tried not to move, the more my body yearned for it, and my refusal kept me from sleeping. My only option was to lay awake, which I did for over an hour until, finally, I drifted back to my dreams.

The alarm clock made me loathe the morning since I hadn't had much sleep, but my bladder forced me out of bed. I was thrilled that we had made it through the night with no issues.

It was Adam's first day back to work since returning home, and his full night's sleep had left him in a positive mood to face the day. He seemed almost excited to be going back to the base. That Thursday morning lent me hope as I dropped the kids off at school and headed to the USO for some volunteer work that I took part in once a month with some other military wives.

"How does it feel to have Adam back home?" One asked.

"Oh, it's so amazing," I responded with a grin. "I miss him so much when he's gone. You know how that is."

"I sure do, honey," the sixty-something wife of an officer replied. "Luckily for us, the older he gets, the less they send him away," she giggled and I looked forward to those days. "It's funny. As much as I love our Marines and military, there were so many years that all I wanted Earl to do was quit, find a job that wasn't so dangerous and kept him at home with the kids and me, but I know that he never would've been happy doing that. The military is his life, his sense of pride. There's truly nothing else that he'd rather do." Adam was the same way. The Marines was his passion and his pride. Being a proud Marine was his identity. He could never see himself doing anything else.

"I know exactly what you mean," I told her. I, too, had spent many nights on my knees, praying to God for his release from the military, for another passion to replace it, but God knew that his job was serving his country. "Can I ask you a personal question, Ava?"

"Of course, honey, anything."

"Has Earl ever struggled with any effects from his tours?" She tilted her head back in thought.

"You know, I think it was just two years ago that he had his last one, but he used to have awful nightmares for days, even weeks, after he came home. He would jerk his body, even yell out sometimes until he woke from it. We never fully know what they go through in those terrible places," she said. "Is Adam having trouble?"

"Yes!" I wanted to cry out, yearning to confide in

someone for advice, but I held silent. I wanted to tell Ava what was going on in hopes that she would offer some wise words that could, somehow, get us through it. I needed someone to tell me that it would all be okay. She was one of the few who still hadn't heard about Adam's capture and rescue. "Just a couple of nightmares," was my response instead. Surely, she would think I was crazy if I told her the truth, how he had nearly ended my life.

Early that evening, after I had run some errands and picked up the kids from school, I was in the kitchen, cooking dinner, when Adam got home.

"Hey, babe," I greeted him. "How was your first day back?" He looked exhausted.

"You know, it's work," he replied sullenly, and I knew something was on his mind.

"Why don't you sit down and relax for a little while," I said. "I'll get you a cold beer."

"Ah, that sounds good. Thanks sweetheart."

Within fifteen minutes, Adam had drifted off to sleep in his cozy recliner, and I stared at his peaceful face. I loved him more than life itself and wished for an end to his agony. The war had cursed him and stolen his contentment. It had plagued him with anguish that tormented him deep down in his soul. I'm ashamed to say that it even made me wonder what he gained from his service in the military. He was sacrificing himself and risking his life only to be tortured in the end. I suppose that he was in it more to give than to receive, and that was what gave him so much pride.

The spaghetti sauce bubbled, gently, on the stove when the kids ran in from outside.

"Is dinner ready yet?" Andrew shouted.

"Sshh, your dad is resting. Keep it down a little," I instructed. "Dinner is almost ready, so go clean up, and take your sister with you."

The four of us sat in our usual spots at the table to say grace before Adam and the kids began gulping down their food, almost too fast for conversation.

"This sauce is the best, babe," my husband complimented.

"Thanks. I used fresh tomatoes from the garden."

"I love it, too, Mommy," little Anabel added.

"Aww, thank you sweetheart," I told her. "Mommy made it special, just for you."

"And Andrew?" She queried.

"Yes, and Andrew too," I replied.

"What about me?" My witty husband joked. "Okay, I made it special for all of you."

Everyone cleared their plates and left the room as quickly as they had entered it.

"I'll help you clean up, babe," Adam said as he gathered the plates from the table. "I love this part of being back home, doing simple things, like you and me cleaning up the dinner dishes together. You don't realize how much the small things mean to you until you're overseas doing it with a bunch of men."

"Well, it must be bad if cleaning up dishes is what you miss," I responded and we laughed. He grabbed my waist, pulling me in to him.

"I missed you," he gazed into my eyes and said, and he kissed me.

While Andrew and Anabel played in their rooms, Adam and I spent our evening on the couch together, wrapped in each other's arms. I was so happy to have him home again, but the approaching night evoked anxiety. I was still worried about what his dreams would bring.

"Last night was fine," I told myself. "It will be okay." Perhaps it was just those first couple of days home that he needed to adjust to.

In bed, we made love and drifted off to sleep in each other's arms.

CHAPTER 4

Hours later, Adam's vacancy in bed awoke me. Only silence infiltrated the darkness, and I found it more troubling than his screams. My heart nearly raced out of my chest and, afraid that turning on the light would startle him, I sat quietly, listening for a clue of where he might be. The pounding of my heart in my chest thrashed violently in my ears and my fear of Adam's hiding, in preparation of an attack, immobilized me where I sat. I was halted in place for ten minutes before I talked myself into turning on the small porcelain lamp next to the bed. The soft illumination revealed his absence.

"Adam," I softly called out in my trembling voice with no answer. "Honey?" The eerie silence remained as I eased, cautiously, out of the covers and down the hallway with my unsteady legs trembling beneath me. My heart was a time bomb as I trekked slowly toward a dim light in the kitchen that we left on each night. "Adam?" I gently called out again, but there was no response. The house appeared void of him after a brief check of each room. I peered out of different windows until I caught a glance of him darting from behind one vehicle to another as if strategically stalking his prey. My heart sank as I could only observe him, sprinting around, completely nude, and I felt hopeless. His condition warranted more than I was capable of handling. Adam needed help from a professional. As I watched him, my eyes overflowed their tears, and I wondered how the war could have reduced such an intellectual man to that. I was desperate to free him of his prison but unsure how. All I could manage, at that moment, were my tears. I knew that I had to go out and get him, but I was terrified to step back into his nightmare.

"Mommy," I heard Anabel groggily utter from behind me and I hastily dried my tears to face her.

"Sweetie, what are you doing up? Is everything

alright?"

"I'm thirsty," she responded, rubbing her tired eyes. I grew tense, praying that I could get her back to sleep before she saw her father.

"I'll get you a drink of water but then right back to bed, okay?" She nodded in agreement.

As our daughter sipped her water, I heard the erratic footsteps of Adam on the porch. In a struggle against my alarm, I hurried Anabel, but her father walked in before I could get her back to her bedroom. For what seemed to me like several seconds, Adam and Anabel stared at each other as if stunned to be meeting. His eyes appeared glazed and vacant while sweat beads doused his ashen forehead. Immediately, he cupped his private area with his hands and ran to our bedroom.

"Why is Daddy naked?" Anabel inquired, and I couldn't muster up a response for anything at that moment. Panic was in control of me because I had no answers. My husband wasn't in his right mind, and I wasn't sure if he even viewed Anabel as his daughter at that moment.

"Uh, well honey, um," I stammered for an answer. "Daddy thought he heard a noise outside and ran out there so quickly that he forgot his pajamas." It was a poor excuse for an explanation, but it was all that I had. I began to laugh it off as if it was a joke and, when she joined in the laughter, I knew that she had accepted my response. "Let's go back to bed."

I was on an emotional roller coaster that I couldn't escape, and I wasn't sure how much more I could take. I felt like I was living with two different men, and I didn't know which would show up at any given time. I returned to the bedroom to find Adam cautiously peering out of various windows, frantically moving from one to another.

"It's alright, honey," I reassured him. "You're safe at home. No one can hurt us."

"Are they coming?" He asked, frantically, and I

stared at him with confusion. "We need to get ready."

"Who is he talking about?" I wondered but, at any rate, I found it safer to just join in his charade.
"No, honey, they're gone. You're at home now.
You're safe."

He continued moving from window to window for nearly twenty more minutes before I could calm his worries.

"You're at home and safe, sweetheart. They're gone," I repeated again and again.

I made some hot tea as he sat at the kitchen table, trying to pull himself together. He insisted on sitting with his back against the wall, and I didn't question it if it was what he needed to feel secure. I watched intently as he looked frequently past me and observed his surroundings, cautiously. His suspicion was beginning to evoke my own.

"We are okay," I insisted, taking his hands in mine.

"I don't know anymore," he answered, breaking down. The only other times I had seen my husband cry were when our two children were born, and his tears traumatized my heart. I planted myself on his lap with his head in my arms, consoling him. It was all I knew to do.

"It's going to be alright, babe," I assured him, holding him tightly. His tears invited mine, but I managed to hold them back to lend strength to him. They seemed to invite reality back.

"I go to sleep and wake up back there," he said, slowly lifting his head. "I can't control it." I could hear the desperation in his voice but I was helpless. "I even tell myself before I go to sleep at night that I won't do it but it still happens. It even happens during the day." I hadn't realized that his episodes occurred during the day, too, but he explained that they were always more prevalent at night. "Damn the war!" He tearfully exclaimed so loudly that I was sure it woke the children. "You go and fight for your country, but no one tells you what happens afterward. No one tells you about this. They just toss you back into civilization." He had always devoted himself, faithfully, to the military but felt that they had let him down.

"I know, honey, but we're going to get you the help that you need," I told him. "Delilah 'says that Kaneohe has a great PTSD program."

Delilah was a neighbor of ours whose husband was also a Marine. She and I had become instant friends, almost from the day we moved to the base. She and Steve were like family to us, and I trusted her completely. We leaned heavily on each other when our husbands were deployed, which was almost always at the same time. Delilah had been forced to familiarize herself with the post-war counseling programs a few years prior, when Steve suffered depression after losing an arm in a tour of duty.

Adam promised me that night, in our kitchen, that he would seek counseling, just as Steve had, and I had to believe that it would all get better. I had made my own promise that if he confided in a therapist, I wouldn't make him talk to me about it.

The next morning, he went to work and I assumed my normal ritual. Outside, the graying clouds suppressed the sun and birthed rain drops on the windshield as I drove the kids to school.

"I wish it was sunny," Anabel commented.

"Me, too, so we could go swimming after school," Andrew added.

"Oh, I'm sure the sun will come out tomorrow," I assured them.

"Hey, that's the song from *Annie*!" My perceptive young daughter recalled, and it made me giggle.

"That song is stupid," Andrew told his sister. "Is not!" She argued.

"It is too and so is that movie!"

"Okay, that's enough!" I finally intervened. "Stop bickering or you're both walking to school." It was another one of my jokes that neither of them found humor in.

"Ha ha, Mom," my daughter sarcastically remarked.

"Yeah, real funny, mother," Andrew added with the insertion of the only title he called me at his age.

"Have a good day," I told them when I stopped at the school, "and Andrew, stop calling me 'mother'."
"Okay, mother," he snickered as he walked away. "I should have gotten a dog," I snickered.

Our family had always thrived on humor, the jokes and little jabs at one another that helped us through the serious times. I needed it more than ever then. On the way back, I called Delilah.

"I don't feel like going home yet," I said. "Let's go out for breakfast. I'll be there in five minutes."

We sat in a little diner, on base, as the rain pounded the road outside. The aromas of freshly-brewed coffee and bacon delighted my nose as the waitresses bustled their way from table to table, taking orders and delivering meals.

"So, how does it feel to have Adam home again? It must have been awful going through what he did over there." She said.

"It was awful, but it's really great having him home," I replied. "I missed him so much, and the kids are thrilled to have him back, of course. How is Steve doing?"

"Better, but it's still day by day," she said. "It's great what they're doing for our country, but this shit is getting old!" Delilah was a no-nonsense kind of woman who always felt, somehow, slighted by the military and had, long ago, lost her faith in the government. "Seems to me that our work over there is done, and a lot of soldiers could have been saved from dying or coming back maimed. Why are they still there? It's time to bring them back home."

"The war doesn't end for them when they get home," I said, staring down into my creamer-lightened coffee as I slowly traced the cup's rim with my thumb. "Adam has been going through some serious things since he came back - flashbacks and nightmares." I was reluctant to publicize our personal struggles, but I needed advice from someone I trusted. "It's like he goes to sleep and is suddenly back in the war, and the worst part is that I'm the enemy." I told Delilah about the things that had been happening at night and about my anxiety because of it. "I'm afraid," I confessed. Her eyes sympathized with me as I released my feelings and concerns.

"Steve went through a little of that, but not to that extreme," she said. "We can't even imagine the stuff they see over there, and we can't expect them to just forget when they come home." She told me about a pact the men had made, in Iraq, not to talk about their experiences back at home. "Adam really should talk to a counselor."

"In fifteen years, Delilah, I've never feared my husband until now. I'm afraid to sleep in the same room with him." Tears flooded my eyes as I spoke of my fears.

"Then don't," she advised, bluntly. "Sleep with the kids, behind locked doors, until Adam gets the help he needs. He'll understand why you have to do that." Delilah made a good point. Our safety was the top priority, and I didn't know if one of Adam's episodes would lead him into our children's bedrooms while I slept. The thought of it terrified me, especially after what had already transpired with Anabel the previous night. Perhaps her suggestion was the solution, at least temporarily, I thought. I had an obligation to protect our children at all costs, even if it was from their own father.

That evening, Adam was late getting home.

"How was your day, honey?" I greeted.

"Not bad," he replied in a bit of an evasion. His suspicious behavior grew evident when he scurried away as I tried to kiss him. He refused to look me in the eye like he normally did when we spoke. I watched as he occupied himself doing small, insignificant things in an apparent attempt to avoid me.

"Is everything alright?" I probed after several minutes.

"Oh yeah, babe, everything's fine." His tone was tender but suspect, all the while, as if he was hiding something.

"Were you able to see the counselor?" I assumed it was his reason for being late.

"Um, no, not yet," he answered. "They're all busy right now, I guess, but I'm still trying." It made sense since so many service members had just returned home.

"Okay," I replied softly. "I just thought that since you were so late…"

"So now I have a curfew?" He huffed, and I was taken aback by his sudden defensiveness.
"No, of course not. I just…"

"What are you accusing me of?"

"Nothing, Adam. Nevermind." Our spat forced me into the bathroom with my tears. I couldn't ever remember a time that my husband had scoffed at me that way, and I had never cried as much, in my entire life as I had since he'd been back from Iraq. I felt like our marriage was in serious trouble.

Adam's outburst had left me flabbergasted. Something was wrong with him that he obviously didn't want to discuss, but I was hurt and incensed by how he was reacting. I wasn't sure what I had done, and I began to replay our interaction in my head for a clue as to what I may have said to provoke his reaction. A light knock, soon, came on the bathroom door.

"Allison, sweetheart," I heard him utter, "I'm sorry." His words lent instantaneous relief, even though he'd said them a hundred times in just two days. "I didn't mean to snap at you." I eased my way out of my small haven to see his apologetic eyes.

"I'm sorry, babe," Adam repeated with his hands on my shoulders. I was staggered by the potency of alcohol on his breath since he'd never been much of a drinker.

"Have you been drinking?" I asked, already clear on the answer. He stood, frozen and vacant with glazed eyes, like a child about to be scolded.

"I had a hectic day so I did stop for a couple of beers," he confessed, cautiously, perhaps expecting my displeasure, but I wasn't upset about it. What bothered me was his apparent need to conceal it from me.

"Okay, I understand," I told him. I couldn't debate the fact that Adam needed something to take the edge off and calm him. The alcohol had evidently succeeded because Adam slept peacefully through the night.

That Saturday morning bestowed relief and a sense of replenishment. The radiant sun promised a glorious day, and I felt a new sense of freedom. I thanked God for his blessing. The house was tranquil with the brilliant rays peeking through the windows and I relished the peace. I loved those quiet mornings, and I thought about how wonderful my life was, how much I adored my family and how lucky I was to have them all. My world was complete and fulfilling. It was all that I could have wanted and more. I was curled up on the couch, watching a movie, when I heard the timid rumblings of Anabel on her way down the hall to greet me. It wasn't long before Andrew followed and the three of us sat, cuddled up together under a blanket, on the couch.

"Are you watching this?" My son probed, as he always did, in a bid to change the channel and, even though I had been, I turned on cartoons for them while I made pancakes and eggs.

"Can you make mine scrambled?" Andrew requested.

"I want mine so I can dip my toast in it," Anabel chimed in.

"Sunny side up?"

"Huh?" Her confusion stepped in.

"That's what the eggs are called when they are made that way," I giggled but she seemed uninterested.

"Can you put jelly on my toast, Mother?"

"Yes, son, but stop calling me 'Mother'!" I ribbed. "What should we do today?" I asked them.

"The beach!" It was always their favorite thing to do, especially for Andrew, who on a dire mission to teach himself to surf. After breakfast, I packed some snacks and drinks, and we headed out to the gleaming, white sand.

The day was supreme with its cloudless sky and gentle sea breeze, soothing my skin with its caress. The ocean seemed especially inviting that day with its luminous, aqua hue, shimmering like glass. As the kids played, I sat on our spacious comforter in the heated sand, breathing in the day's glory and feeling blessed for the serenity it granted me, as if God was telling me that everything would be okay.

"Dad's trying to surf again," Anabel giggled. "Yeah, and he keeps wiping out," her brother joined in.

"Are you okay, honey?" I yelled to him as he nearly drowned in his struggle to stay on the surfboard. He was in the water more than on the board, and the three of us couldn't contain our laughter. Adam gave the thumbs up and fell back into the water. "Andrew, you might have to go save your father before he drowns."

"Yeah, and teach him how to surf," Anabel added.

I relished those days, when we had nothing to do but be together as a family, enjoying one another and having a good time. They were priceless to me and there was nowhere else that I would have rather been. I gazed at the majestic mountains in the distance and statuesque palm trees that surrounded us. It had to be the most beautiful place on earth, I thought, and it gave us a well-needed vacation from our struggles.

CHAPTER 5

As the days passed, Adam's drinking grew increasingly more evident, but I knew that it helped him sleep. It became his ritual to drink two beers each night before bed and, even though his method had halted his episodes, I wondered why he hadn't bothered to consult the therapist rather than drinking himself to sleep each night. I couldn't complain about something that was working, but I hoped it wasn't his way of masking his problem.

Adam and I had planned a night out with Delilah and Steve on the following weekend, which we did once a month. The four of us enjoyed dressing up for a leisurely night on the town, without the children, for dinner, dancing and good conversation. My crimson silk dress made me feel exquisite, and I complimented it with the diamond necklace and bracelet from Adam that I only wore on special occasions.

"Mommy, you look pretty," Anabel graciously complimented.

"Thank you, sweetheart," I replied with a gracious grin. "Jessica, thanks for staying with them, and call if you have any problems," I told the teenaged sitter. I was looking forward to a relaxed night out.

The restaurant was serene with soft lighting and fine art ornamenting its gold-colored walls. Every table was adorned with white linen and candle light. The four of us began our evening with a bottle of Pinot Noir.

"A toast," Adam lifted his glass, "to good food and great friends."

"Here here," Deliliah replied as we all raised our glasses.

"It's nice to have you back home, man," Steve told Adam.

"It's great to be back," he replied. "Now, I have to

get started on that honey-do list," he grinned with a wink in my direction.

"It never ends. Mine is growing by the day!" Steve joked.

"Yeah, I'm sure that lying on the couch is excruciating for you," Delilah rebutted, evoking laughter from the rest of us.

Throughout dinner, Adam appeared to be drinking more than usual, and he was growing more boisterous by the hour.

"Honey, you're being a little loud," I told him amidst the stares from the other patrons around us.

"What? We're just having a good time," he responded, unconcerned. "Let's have another bottle of wine." We had already opened our second.

"Why don't we dance?" I suggested as the mellow piano music was played.

"Alright, babe, let's go." He staggered out of his chair with his hand out to me and led me to the dance floor. "Are you having a good time?" He inquired with slurred speech as we danced.

"Yes, of course," I answered, "but, honey, can you tone it down a bit until we leave here?"

"Am I being too loud? I'm sorry." 'Sorry' seemed to be his favorite word.

The four of us chose to cap off our evening at a local bar.

"Babe, I'm ready to dance!" Adam merrily announced, and we laughed at his comedic attempt.

"Is he dancing or trying to hula hoop?" I teased.

"Why is it that every guy who gets drunk suddenly thinks he can dance?" Delilah ribbed.

"Just don't let him sing," I joked.

"Let's get a round of shots!" Adam bought us each a shot of tequila and then another. "Come on, babe," he said, leading me to the dance floor. It was a side of my husband that I had only seen a couple of times, before our kids were born, and I had truly missed his frivolous humor. I laughed as we danced the night away, and it was the most fun that I could remember having together in years. "I love you," he said as we danced.

"I love you, too, crazy man," I replied and Adam climbed up onto a chair.

"Hey, everybody!" He yelled out to the patrons in the bar. "This crazy man is wildly in love with this stunning woman!" His announcement evoked the roaring cheers of everyone around as I grinned from ear to ear with flattery.

"We should get him drunk more often," Delilah commented with a grin.

From there, Adam's drinking seemed to progress. It wasn't just one or two beers before bed anymore. He began drinking from the minute he came home from work, each evening, until he went to bed at night, and it was neither paced nor casual. He drank like it was a party, until he was drunk enough to sleep. Maybe it was his way of burying his scars from Iraq or, perhaps, it just numbed the truth. I found myself at a crossroads, comparing the drinking and the flashbacks and pondering which of the two evils I preferred. One was as bad as the other. Alcohol masked his pain and his ability to cope with it and, as long as he could just drink his problems away, he didn't see a need to pursue any other method.

Andrew and Anabel dubbed their father more fun and lenient but it was I who reaped the consequences, the agony of watching my husband self-destruct. He wasn't the same person anymore. I was sleeping with a stranger at night, reluctantly accommodating his increased sex drive and hacking the overbearing odor of alcohol on his breath as he slept. It was I who assumed what were always his responsibilities around the house, like mowing the lawn and washing the vehicles, because he was too drunk to do them. It became that the only time he wasn't drinking was when he was at work. I wondered if it was more tolerable to risk Adam's flashbacks of the war or cope with the effects of an alcoholic. He desperately needed help.

The phone rang, one evening, and I answered it to hear his father's voice. Adam's parents lived in Colorado and called a few times a month. For weeks, I had been making excuses for why their son wasn't available to speak to them. I didn't want to compromise my husband's dignity in front of his parents, and I didn't want them to feel the desperation that I felt in the midst of his inebriated ramblings. I felt the usual flutter in my heart, dreading yet another invented excuse for why their son wasn't able to speak to them. Adam's father inquired how the kids and I were, as he always did, and then asked the question.

"Is my son around tonight?" I hesitated, knowing that I couldn't continue the charade like the dutiful wife that my husband expected me to be. I couldn't withhold Adam from his parents any longer, even if we felt it was protecting them from the harsh reality.

"I need to tell you something first," I stammered, hesitantly. I wanted to prepare my father-in-law for what he would soon discover. "Adam has been drinking a little this evening." My concocted tale was that his son had merely had a stressful day at work. I still couldn't bear to admit the truth and disappoint the people who were so adoring and proud of their only child.

"Hey, Dad," Adam cheerfully slurred. His father must have begun his interrogation, almost immediately, because he followed it up with, "yeah, I've had a few." After a brief conversation, he handed the phone back to me.

"He's three sheets to the wind," my father-in-law said. "I didn't think he drank like that."

"I think it's just been an unusually rough day," I fibbed, certain that he could see through my facade. "I'll get him in bed." I was disgusted with myself for lying to Adam's parents like I had, even though I felt I had done it to spare them the pain that I coped with each night. "From now on, Adam, you're calling them before you start drinking," I insisted. "I'm not lying for you anymore."

"Babe, come have a drink with me." His words were insistent and garbled.

"Not right now," I replied, trying desperately to mask my irritation. I was tired of living with a drunk and frustrated that we couldn't carry on an intelligent conversation anymore. He wanted me to join his never ending party, but one of us still had to bear responsibility.

"Come on, Al, relax with me." If he had his way, I would have been sitting there, drinking with him every night, and he had a way of making me feel guilty that I didn't, almost as if I wasn't any fun anymore.

"No, Adam, I won't because one of us still has to be responsible. I'm tired of seeing you like this every night, and it has to stop."

"I'm not hurting anyone. I'm not breaking any laws. I'm serving my country and I just want to relax when I get home", he rationalized.

"You are hurting someone, Adam," I huffed. "Me. I can't do this anymore."

"What are you saying?" He slurred.

"You need help," I insisted, "counseling, not alcohol, and if you don't stop, the kids and I are leaving." The last thing I wanted was to leave my husband and separate our family, but I would be left with no other option if he didn't get the help that he needed.

"Babe, don't leave," he pleaded in a stupor. "Don't leave me. I need you. Please, Al, stay with me. I'll do anything. We're supposed to be forever."

"Yes, and you're supposed to be sober." I drew closer with my hands on his cheeks and my insistent eyes glaring into his. "This family needs you. We need you to be strong and healthy, and so does the military." His eyes closed and he leaned his head back with a deep breath, absorbing my words.

"I know," he said. "I've been taking the easy road, and it's time to get back on track." I was so relieved to hear him say it, but part of me wondered how much of his agreement was merely to halt the conversation.

"I'll help you every way that I can," I assured him. "We'll get through it."

I prayed that his vow was authentic, yearning to have back the man that I married. We knew that we had a long and demanding road ahead, but I was sure that it would be worth it in the end. I was willing to do whatever it took to have my husband back. Without Adam's drinking, I had to prepare myself for the inevitable return of his flashbacks, the soldier that endlessly stalked his prey, and I feared the unexpected. I wondered what I would do if his nightmares grew worse, how I would keep defending and protecting myself and our children, but all we could hope for was that the counseling would help him.

Adam followed through on his promise throughout the next day, with no alcohol. I noticed how difficult it was for him as he struggled to keep himself busy through the evening to avoid his habit, and I was proud of his attempt.

"Let's go for a walk on the beach," I suggested to him as an offer to help occupy his mind, "or we could watch a movie." Neither option lent any appeal to him so

I continued to watch him pace, endlessly, around the house and outside. That night, I crawled into bed with a pit of anxiety breeding in my stomach, fearful of how I would be awakened.

"Would you feel better sleeping with the kids?" My concerned husband asked me. "I would understand." I recalled Delilah's advice to do just that, and the thought was tempting, but I couldn't leave Adam on his own.

"I'm okay," I assured him and drifted off to sleep in the security of his arms.

The alarm clock read 2:19 a.m. when I awoke to Adam's rustling in bed. Only a few sporadic words were audible within his continuous mumbling and tossing, but they were evidence of a horrific dream.

"Stop it!" he uttered. "Let him go."

I was afraid to shake him for fear of his actions, but I needed to intervene before it progressed. My trembling hand refused to steady itself as I reached out to his shoulder, and I questioned if it was better to cuddle him, instead, so that he might know it was me, his wife, rather than the enemy. My muscles threatened to freeze and I took a deep breath.

"Honey," I called to him, softly, with no contact at all. "Sweetheart."

"No," he murmured in a sudden shift of motion, and it caused me to back away.

"Maybe I should get out of bed for this," I thought, in case he lunged at me again, but I didn't. "Honey," I repeated with a gentle shake of his arm. Adam rolled toward me with a swift push, knocking me to the floor, and I found myself laughing because of it. I picked myself up from the carpet, determined to try again as his muttering continued. "Honey," I echoed from beside of the bed.

"Az," he garbled, almost as if calling out for

someone. "Az." I hadn't a clue what it meant but Adam repeated it several times. His face told a story of anguish, and his squinted eyes were dewy. His dream held an obvious despondency, and I wondered what the vision was.

"Honey," I beckoned louder, and Adam's soaked eyes opened amid his heavy breath. Relief encompassed him as he peered, cautiously, at his surroundings in the glow of the television. He appeared to be wrestling with bewilderment. "It was just a dream," I said, caressing his sweat-beaded forehead. He held me, tightly, in his arms, seemingly with appreciation of the comforts of home. Gradually, his hammering heart calmed and his breathing slowed as he drifted back to sleep.

Adam didn't seem to remember his dream the next day or, if he did, he wouldn't admit it, but it seemed to me that a nightmare so vivid would have provoked at least some recollection of it. Maybe it was just that he preferred not to talk about it.

"You kept saying 'Az'," I told him.

"I did?" He sounded stunned that I had spoken the word.

"Is that a place or something?"

"A person," he responded, hesitantly, clearing his throat. "I can't really talk about this right now," he added, and I could see that it was a sensitive subject.

"Okay, well, don't forget about Anabel's school play tonight." I wasn't willing to force his vision back on him.

"Sure thing," he replied. "I'll be home in plenty of time." He left for work,and I finished sewing our daughter's costume before starting the housework. The brilliant sun warmed the earth outside, and I couldn't wait to delve into my flower gardens of Oahu's most vibrant. I had never seen more magnificent floral masterpieces than the stunning tropicals of Hawaii. Gardening was my haven from the outside world, where the dense and multi-colored plants of orange, pink and yellow enveloped me in its own sanctity, away from reality's plagues. It was my favorite escape.

The confines of my comfortable garden felt safe and offered the solace that I desperately desired. With my hands obscured in the cool, spongy soil, I thought about Adam and our marriage. I thought about our children. My family was my entire world and, up until then, our unity seemed resilient, almost as if we were immune from the issues that other families endured. Our harmonious life together had always seemed to deflect any obstacles but, for the first time ever, I found myself questioning the security of it. Our safeguarded family was no more. For only a moment, I envisioned Adam and me living separate lives, sharing our children, individually, at separate times, spending holidays apart and broken, and I had never done that before. My heart nearly ceased pulsing at the thought of living without him.

"There's my gorgeous wife," Adam greeted after work that evening.

"And there is my handsome husband." I walked over to kiss him. "How was your day?"

As a housewife, I always made it a point to ask about my husband's day, have the house clean and dinner waiting for him. It wasn't that I was a submissive, old- fashioned woman, but it was the least that I could do for a hero like him who gave all that he had, everyday, for the people of our country.

Adam was a true American, a proud Marine who devoted himself, completely, to the United States Military. There was no order he wouldn't obey and no criticism of it that he would tolerate. He served with complete dedication, every minute. It didn't stop when he returned home from work or from a tour of duty. He was a Marine all the time, faithfully upholding the honor, and putting on the uniform boasted of his pride.

"Daddy!" Anabel ran to her father's arms when she heard his voice.

"Hi pumpkin. How's my baby girl today?" He said, sweeping her off the floor. "What did you do today, bud?" Adam asked our son at the dinner table.

"Nothing, really," he said, "just boring stuff at school."

"These are the best times of your life, Andy, so enjoy them," Adam advised.

"How is school the best time of my life?" He huffed. "I'd rather work and get paid."

"Well, son, that will come in time. Don't rush it," his father told him. "We're still on for the Padres game tomorrow night, right?"

"You know it!" Andrew exclaimed. Sports was a passion that the two of them shared together. It was something that they had, just between the two of them, and Andrew relished the time with his mentor.

"Don't forget about my school play at seven," Anabel reminded him.

"About that," he responded. "I don't think I'll be able to make it tonight, baby girl." Adam peered at the floor with guilt as displeasure assaulted me.

"Why not?" I hoped that he had a valid excuse, at least, because I could already see our daughter's obvious disappointment.

"I have to pull some extra duty at work tonight," he said. "I can't get out of it. I'm sorry, Ana."

It wouldn't be Anabel's first school function that I had attended without her father, given his number of tours overseas, but while he was home, she expected Adam to be there. We both did. Even still, it was understood that the military took precedence, whether we liked it or not.

"Well, if duty calls then you have to go," I told

him.

I hoped that Anabel would understand. After dinner, I called Delilah.

"How would you like to go see a play?" She couldn't replace Adam, but Anabel would enjoy the extra applause.

With Andrew in tow, we found our seats in the dimly-lit school auditorium, awaiting the elementary rendition of *The Farmer in the Dell.*

"This is exciting," my friend remarked with a grin.

"Ana is the chicken," my son chimed in, humored at the vision of his sister being poultry.

"The hen," I corrected with a giggle.

"Well, the hen is the best animal on the farm. Without her, there would be no eggs," Delilah said with a smile and we both chuckled. "So, why couldn't Adam make it?" She casually queried in her raspy tone.

"He said he had to pull some extra duty at work." "Really? Hmm…"

"What?" Her dubious response demanded my attention.

"Nothing," she said.

"No, what is it?" My curiosity was getting the best of me.

"Well, I don't want to start any trouble here, but there is no extra duty this month." I was taken aback by her words. Adam wouldn't lie to me about that, I thought, but with Steve serving in the same unit, surely Delilah knew.

"That can't be right," I replied with perplexity. There has to be some kind of misunderstanding."

"I don't think so, Al," she responded, timidly. "I specifically remember Steve telling me how happy all of the guys were about it." Neither Delilah nor Adam had any reason to lie to me so it had to be a misunderstanding, I assumed, but it was still enough to make me wonder if there was something else going on.

"…And this farm has the most beautiful animals around," I heard, and my thoughts were suspended to see Anabel take the stage with her classmates, all dressed up as farm animals and each reciting two or three short lines in the performance. I watched, proudly, with glorious eyes and a grin, at my daughter's flawless portrayal.

"I'm the hen," she recited, "and my job on the farm is to lay eggs for the farmer and his family to eat. My role is important because my eggs are also sold to local markets for people to buy."

"Aw, isn't she the best hen ever?" I boasted.

"Definitely the best I've ever seen," Delilah agreed. After the show, we congratulated the cast on their performance.

"I wish Daddy could have been here," Anabel said.

"I know, sweetheart, me too, but I videotaped it for him to see," I told her.

"I think I'm ready for show business," she so proudly announced, sending the rest of us into an eruption of laughter.

That night, I waited up for Adam to get home. Delilah's words had engraved themselves into my head, and my suspicion about his whereabouts that evening continued to grow. I hoped that my husband hadn't lied to me, but I needed confirmation. It wasn't until after eleven when he finally walked through the door. He looked fatigued and worn out.

"I thought you'd be in bed by now," he said. "How was the play?"

"It was good. Anabel was the best talking hen that I've ever seen," I replied. "How was work?"

"Oh well, you know, uneventful," he babbled, and it only fed my fears. I didn't want to assume anything or make accusations, but I couldn't deny his odd behavior.

"Are you hungry?"

"Actually, just really tired so I think I'm just going to hit the sack. Tell Anabel that her daddy is proud."

CHAPTER 6

Adam's demeanor, that night, was uncharacteristic of himself, but I wondered how much of it was my own suspicion. Perhaps I was paranoid and just looking for something that he might have done wrong. I wanted so much to believe that Adam had been at work, as he had declared, but his story just didn't add up.

I woke up the next morning, pleasantly surprised that Adam had slept through the night, and I felt refreshed. Mornings were my favorite time of the day. Even though he didn't have to be at work until noon, he was already up and the splendid aroma of brewing coffee overflowed the house.

The kitchen windows summoned in the soothing sun and it was one of my most savored things, comforting me in its warmth. As I poured myself a cup of coffee, I caught a glimpse of Adam sitting on the deck, staring out at the bay. I wanted to question him about the previous night, but I opted instead to leave him alone with his thoughts and took the kids to school.

"Morning, babe," he greeted with a peck on my cheek. "I didn't know you were back," he said when he came in for a refill of his coffee. "Come out on the deck with me. It's beautiful out today."

"You looked like you were in deep thought so I didn't want to disturb you." He motioned for me to sit on his lap.

"You can disturb me anytime, baby doll. You're my favorite interruption," he told me, sweetly.

I sat on his lap, with his arms wrapped around me, admiring the sun's radiant reflection on the water of the Kaneohe Bay, and I swore that it was the most exquisite place in the world. I never wanted to be anywhere else.

Adam's embrace felt safe, shielding me from the rest of the world and vowing to always protect me. He held me close to him, almost as if we were connected and, from the corner of my eye, I saw his doting gaze.

"You are so beautiful," he complimented, looking at me, adoringly, as if in awe of the vision.

"It's because you make me happy," I told him with a fluttering heart.

"I love you so much, Allison. There's not a day that I don't thank God for giving me this amazing family. You're my reason for living." His sincerity induced my tears, especially given what we had been going through.

"And you're mine," I echoed. I couldn't even put into words how much he truly meant to me. I loved Adam more than life, and our marriage was sacred to me. There was nothing I wouldn't do for my family.

"It's hard to believe that we'll be celebrating fifteen years together next week," he remarked of our approaching anniversary. "It doesn't seem like it's been that long."

"It seems like an eternity to me," I joked and he began tickling my side, relentlessly, until I laughed so hard I could hardly catch my breath. I playfully pinched his nipple and broke free, provoking him to chase me down the steps and through the yard as we frolicked with laughter.

"You better hope I don't catch you, girl," Adam ribbed.

"I'm not worried," I replied, breathlessly, with a chuckle. "Come and get me, you big, bad Marine!"

Adam chased me through the yard until he tackled me in the dewy grass as we roared with laughter.

"You want to go back to bed?" He suggested, seductively.

"Let's go." As soon as my words were uttered, I saw Delilah and Steve on the deck.

"What are you doing?" She called out to us.

"Foreplay," Adam joked as we walked up the steps, "which you just ruined for me," he ribbed while she shook her head in laughter.

"Maybe later?" I remarked to my husband and he

winked.

"I can see how much fun you're having here, but I came to hitch a ride to work with you today," Steve told him. "Our car battery died."

"Again? Didn't you just replace that?" I asked.

"Yep, just last month," Delilah replied with disgust. "Can you believe it?"

"Of course I'll give you a ride, man."

"Great, thanks. I'll see you in a couple hours." Delilah called me, that afternoon.

"So, did you find out what's going on with Adam?" She probed. "Did he really work last night?"

"No, he definitely didn't work," I answered. "I think he was drinking again. He came home, mumbled a few words and rushed off to bed. He didn't even try to… you know." I sighed. "I don't know what to do anymore. He promised to see a therapist and didn't, he promised to stop drinking and didn't, and I even threatened to leave him, so what now?"

"Well, I think if you're going to threaten, then you need to make good on them," she advised. "Find your bottom line and stick with it." I knew she was right. "You guys looked pretty happy this morning."

"That's the worst part of all," I said. "He got up, in a great mood, as if nothing happened."

"Maybe, to him, nothing did," she said.

Adam was an incredible father to our children. He did more than the average dad, making sure to set aside time for them, doing special things with each one of them, like playing ball, surfing or wrestling with Andrew, or having a tea party with Anabel and her dolls. Adam took the time with them to show that he was truly interested in them and their lives. I relished how wonderful he was with our kids and even wished that my own father had done the same thing growing up.

In my childhood, my father was a figurehead who

was demanding and stern. I came from an old-fashioned upbringing where my father worked, my mother served him and the children were seen and not heard. In fact, the only conversations my father ever really had with us were at the dinner table, where he occasionally asked how school was or what we did that day. Most of the time, he was just the disciplinarian. He rarely smiled and, in most cases, I think he was just making conversation more than that he truly cared about the responses we gave. Most of his time was spent relaxing in his recliner while my mother cooked, ironed clothes or cleaned up the house. My older brother and I were left to entertain ourselves. Adam's childhood was much different. His parents were always very attentive to him. He shared a very close bond with his father, so much so that his mother was often the outcast. My husband was the perfect blend of both of our fathers, and our children adored him.

I was left, still wondering about Adam's actions the night before, why Steve hadn't worked but Adam had, if Adam was really even there. I never wanted to doubt him, but I couldn't rationalize his explanation in my mind.

"Dad, can you take me down to the beach to surf today?" Andrew asked him the following Saturday morning.

"Of course I will. I could use some practice," he responded. "Get that sweet bikini on, babe!" He joked with a pat on my butt.

"Oh yuck!" Our son chimed in, once again annoyed by our flirting.

"Be glad you have parents who are still in love with each other," I told him.

"That's right," Adam concurred. "You can only hope that you find love like this when you're older. Your mother is still the girl of my dreams, after fifteen years."

"And you are still the man of mine," I said to him with a kiss.

"Gross," Andrew remarked as Anabel giggled, grabbing her yellow, plastic bucket and shovel.

"Maybe later, you'll show me what's under the bikini," my grinning husband whispered, and his comment lit my soul ablaze.

At the beach, I assisted Anabel in her splendid sandcastle creations as Adam and our son braved the swollen white waves on their surfboards, frequently being swallowed up by the audacious sea. I chuckled as they fought to stay on the boards only to be heaved back into the water. It wasn't long before the waterlogged pair wandered back to our blanket.

"I'm getting beat up out there," Adam panted.

"I can tell," I ribbed.

"Come on, Dad," Andrew summoned, "let's go back in."

"Go ahead, buddy," he said. "I need to take a little breather."

"I'll go," Anabel offered.

"Stay in the shallow part and be careful," I instructed. "Andy, stay close to your sister."

"You don't know how to surf," I heard Andrew tell his sister as they tread toward the sea.

"I do so," she rebutted in yet another spat between them.

"Alone, at last," Adam ogled and planted a passionate kiss on my lips that sent a flutter through my heart. "You're so hot," he praised in his usual flirtatious manner. "I love you so much, baby doll."

"I love you, too, handsome," I responded, and I meant it with everything I had.

"Come on, Dad," Andrew summoned from the water.

"I guess that's my cue." Adam and I, both, joined the kids in the turquoise water.

That evening, after dinner, my husband disappeared

into the garage while I straightened up the house and, once the kids were asleep a few hours later, he and I retired to our bedroom.

"I've been wanting you all day," he said, pulling me close. He kissed me slowly and softly, the way that he did when we first met, igniting my desires.

"I'll be right back," I said, moving into the bathroom to put on the white, silk and lace lingerie that I had hidden in the cabinet to surprise him. I spritzed on his favorite perfume, fluffed my hair and opened the bathroom door to a room of candlelight and soft music. Red rose petals led to the bed, where champagne and a rose awaited me.

"Wow," he remarked at my appearance.

"I could say the same," I replied of his romantic efforts. Adam lay on his side, the flame's radiance accenting his bronzed and chiseled arms and chest, his inviting eyes seducing me. I never could resist his physical perfection, tactically flaunted before me. I was already turned on just looking at him.

"You look so amazing in that," he complimented as I walked slowly toward him. I was on fire, starved for his touch, and I felt like I would explode with ecstasy at his very first caress.

He handed me a glass of champagne, but I didn't need the prequel to my reward.

"A toast," he said, holding out his glass, "to the most stunning woman I've ever seen."

"And to the most amazing man I've ever known," I added. We sat our glasses down and united in a passionate kiss that delighted my entire body to its core, and his hand made its way, leisurely, up my quivering thigh. I yearned for its progression but he halted just in time. His caresses took over my body, tempting an explosion with every gentle stroke, as if in slow motion. Softly, with his hand behind my head, he lay me before him, a paradise to be discovered.

"You're so exquisite," he said, gazing down at me as my body pleaded to be touched.

He hovered atop of me, barely skimming his loin against mine in a tantalizing game that evoked erotic whimpers from both of us. Adam's satin lips caressed my neck and lobe.

"I need you so bad," he whispered in my ear, and I wasn't sure how much longer I could stand to be without his body on mine. Slowly, his mouth explored my body, working its way down until his tongue found my Eden, evoking a fiery response. I arched my back to offer more as his tongue danced joyously. My moans grew louder in my breathlessness until I couldn't take another stroke. I screamed out as my body quaked with ecstasy. Adam continued in his quest to please me and, almost immediately, my desperate yearning returned. I needed him inside of me, my soaked rapture pleading for him.

I sat up, offering to return the favor to him as he was on his knees, his head fallen back, relishing my attention until he halted it. He lay down and lifted me back to his mouth for a second eruption before thrilling me with his firm appendage. In unison, our bodies danced with one another, blissfully craving the other as if they couldn't get close enough. Joyous gratification took over as we made love, his hips moving, harmonically, with mine, until I felt the climax build through my body, sending it into a quiver of pleasure that controlled my entire being. Together, Adam and I screamed out, boldly, with delight.

My body had never undergone such earth-shattering passion, as if its very blood had just been replenished. My muscles were stone, nearly incapable of movement from the erotic rush that had just taken place.

"God, that was incredible!" My smiling husband complimented. "I think it was the best we've ever had." I had to agree. Never could I recall that level of pleasure before.

"You were amazing." I had to admit that not all of our lovemaking held orgasmic rewards for me and, in fact, I considered myself a bit hard to please in that realm, but never was there a time with Adam that I didn't enjoy it.

The silence of the night brought forth the familiar groans and whimpers of my husband, enrapt in yet another nightmare. His tensed body shuddered and reeled until it shook our bed.

"No!" He yelled out as he quaked. "Help him!"

I envisioned a horrendous scene of his fellow men, helplessly falling prey to bombs and gunfire. I needed to offer escape from his terror and, when I shook him gently, as I often did, piercing screams erupted from him and he leaped out of our bed.

"It's Allison, your wife," I insisted, trying to calm his fears. "It's me, Adam."

Whether he comprehended my words or not is still a mystery because he took cover in the bathtub in our bathroom, curled up and trembling.

"Please, God, no," he prayed. "No, God. Help us." I was afraid of intervening again, for fear of his reaction, but I knew that I needed to.

"I love you, Adam," I said. "It's Allison."

"Help him," he pleaded, and I assumed that he was referring to a wounded soldier.

"I will help him," I assured, hoping that my voice would, somehow, calm him. "Come with me, and we'll help him."

Suddenly, my husband began snoring, as if he had drifted away from his fantasy world and back into a peaceful slumber. Relief encompassed me as I softly woke him.

"Come back to bed, sweetheart," I said as his confusion set in.

"Why am I in the tub?" It would have been comical

had I not just experienced the down side of it all.

"You were taking a bath," I joked, leading him back to bed.

"Okay," he casually replied. My explanation had satisfied him.

CHAPTER 7

Our anniversary was the following week, and we got a sitter to watch the kids for the evening. Adam had made dinner reservations at the best restaurant in Honolulu, and I was anxious to spend a relaxed evening alone with him.

I donned a slinky, blue satin dress with heels and swept my hair gently up, the way that he liked.

"You look incredible," he complimented, seemingly unable to turn his stare away.

"Well, thanks, babe," I replied. "So do you."

He stood, handsomely, in his navy blue suit, which fit so well that it looked like it was tailored solely to him. He was freshly shaven and smelled of my favorite cologne, and his dark, layered hair sported a damp look. I wondered how I had landed such an attractive man. Adam pulled me close to him, gazing into my eyes as I breathed him in.

"I'm so lucky to have you," he remarked. "You're still the girl of my dreams, my heartbeat, and I still want to give you everything I have. I love you with all my heart and soul." His words were the sweetest song to my ears.

"I love you, too, babe, so much," I replied. "You are my life, and I never want to be without you."

"So, you'll take me for another fifteen years?"

"You know I will," I told him. "Happy anniversary, hubby."

"Happy anniversary to you, my lovely wife." His lips on mine sent my heart racing. "Mmm, you smell so good," he said. "I just want to take you right here."

His soft lips traced my neck and chills conquered my body. I wanted him, too, yearning for his touch. Adam's hand found its way under my dress and lifted my leg to his hip as he pressed his weight against me, passionately kissing my lips.

"You're so sexy," he commented in a seductive

whisper, and my body tingled with anticipation.

He slipped his fingers, strategically, under my lace panties, evoking my whimper. They were soon replaced by his mouth and I cried out with pleasure. I released the bulge from his pants and he lifted me onto him. My rhythmic grind grew, gradually, faster, the two of us starved for each other until, only minutes later, an erotic explosion.

"Wow! You're a wild man lately," I joked with my husband. I didn't know what had come over him, but I enjoyed his newfound spontaneity. I couldn't deny that we had, previously, fallen into routines in our marriage, the same thing day in and day out, so I welcomed the change in Adam.

The restaurant in Honolulu was pristine with its ceramic floors and soft lighting. Bouquets of roses complimented fine white linen and candlelight on each cozy table as a piano player offered up his best romantic ballads. We were seated next to a window that displayed the brilliant silhouette of the sea kissing the mountains in the setting sun.

"This view is so incredible that it could be framed art," I remarked in awe of its beauty.

"Just like you," Adam complimented with a gaze. He ordered a bottle of the establishment's finest champagne.

"This is wonderful, honey. Thank you so much." I knew that whole fine dining experience was more for me than for him. He would have been just as content at a buffet or simple steakhouse so I appreciated his effort. "A toast," I said, lifting my glass, "to fifteen amazing years together and still feeling like the luckiest girl in the world."

"To fifteen incredible years of bliss with my sweetheart." He kissed my hand and smiled.

A formally-clad waiter soon appeared with a bouquet of vivid white, long-stemmed orchids.

"For you, from Mr. Koehley," he said.

"Wow, honey, you remembered my favorite flower." His romantic gestures were impressive.

"They are exactly like your wedding bouquet." I was astonished, fighting my moistening eyes. The small card inside of the bouquet read, *Still stunning, 15 years later.*

"You are so amazing," I said to Adam with a kiss. "I can't believe you still remember that. Thank you, babe."

We enjoyed a cuisine of fresh lobster, talking and laughing together as if on our first date again, and it felt wonderful. I gazed at my husband, his striking features and alluring eyes, his captivating smile, wondering how I'd gotten so lucky to have his love. I knew that a man like him could have his choice of women, but I was incredibly thankful that he had chosen me.

The waiter brought a small, beautifully decorated cake to our table to finish off our meal and, on top, I spotted the petite, golden gift box. Adam's eyes followed mine as I reached for it.

"I hope you like it," he uttered softly. With anticipation, I opened the small jewelry box, slowly, as not to appear too eager. Inside was a magnificent band of entwined white gold and diamonds that stole my breath, the radiant jewels reflecting in my astounded eyes.

"It's stunning," I reveled in its beauty, unable to turn away from staring at it.

"It's an anniversary band," he said. "Try it on."

I felt almost like Cinderella, slipping on the glass slipper. The ring embraced my finger perfectly as if it was made just for me. I admired its luminous glimmer under the restaurant's light, in awe of the way that its exquisiteness complimented my finger.

"I love it, babe," I told him. "Thank you so much."

"I do have one more surprise," Adam confessed.

"You've already done enough." I wondered what could possibly be left. In the window next to us, my husband gave a wave and vibrant island lights came on below with our cheering friends waving up at us. My eyes grew wide as I peered down from the pane.

"May I escort you to our anniversary party, Mrs. Koehley?" I was stunned. Adam had truly gone above and beyond to make our day special. Each new surprise managed to top the one before.

"Of course I will," I answered. "I can't believe that you did all of this, Adam." I wondered when he had found the time to plan it all and, furthermore, I felt guilty for my suspicions of his actions when, in truth, he had striven to present me with an unforgettable night.

"It pales in comparison of what you do, babe, for me and for the kids. You deserve this."

We walked downstairs and out onto the beach, where a luau was being held in our honor.

"Happy anniversary!" The crowd cheered. Gathered together were all of our friends from the base and even our parents, who had flown to Hawaii to surprise me.

"Mom, Dad!" I greeted them with a hug, thrilled to see them. "I'm so happy you're here. I can't believe it!" I embraced Adam's parents also. "When did you all get here?"

"We all flew in yesterday," my father-in-law answered.

"Adam put us up in a nice hotel on the beach for a few days," my mother added. I couldn't believe how much thought and effort Adam had put into our anniversary. He had truly thought of everything and I couldn't imagine any better.

"I can't believe you did all of this," I told my grinning husband, greatly impressed by his initiative.

"I wanted to make it really special," he said, and I hugged him with appreciation. He had done that and more.

"Thank you so much, honey. This is truly perfect. I couldn't have asked for anything better."

The beach was lit up with torches that illuminated multi-colored tropical flowers everywhere. I put one in my hair, in true Hawaiian style. A band played Hawaiian music while hula dancers entertained us. Throughout the evening, I made my way through the herd of our friends and family, relishing time with each and every one of them. We talked and laughed, we drank and danced the night away. My intermittent glances at Adam revealed him gradually sinking into a drunken stupor and, though I didn't want to spoil his fun, I feared him going too far, especially in front of his parents.

"Honey, I love that you're having fun, but maybe you should slow down a little bit," I suggested to him.

"Babe, it's a party, our party," he said. "We're celebrating us." He threw his arm around my neck and was nearly hanging on me.

"I know, and I'm glad you're having fun, but I don't want you to get too drunk to function. I want to have a good time with our friends and family tonight."

"We are having a good time. I'm having a great time," he slurred.

"Please, honey, just slow down some, okay?" I felt guilty, lecturing my husband like a child, especially after the evening he had given me for our anniversary. I didn't want to come off as the nagging wife who hampered the fun, but I also didn't want Adam to behave in a way that he would regret in the morning.

"Is he alright?" His concerned father asked me. His eyes spoke of disappointment in his son.

"Yeah, I think he's just having a little too much fun," I explained as if it was nothing. "He's okay." Adam's erratic behavior was making it difficult for me to enjoy the party. I felt the need to look after him so that he didn't embarrass himself. Still, his belligerence gained control.

"Who wants to go swimming?" He called out to the crowd. "Let's all go skinny-dipping!"

I scanned the sea of flabbergasted faces to see both humor and despair as he removed his shirt and hinted at his pants.

"Adam!" I scolded. "Stop it. No one wants to go swimming."

"Al, everyone wants to go skinny-dipping," he insisted with a grin of amusement. He pulled the remainder of his clothes off and stood, completely nude, in front of our guests, some snickering and others embarrassed.

"Look at our parents," I commanded softly. "Do they look amused right now?" Our parents appeared mortified by Adam's antics and so was I.

"They need to loosen up and have some fun," he rebutted.

"Please put your clothes back on before you ruin our anniversary," I pleaded with desperation.

"Oh, because you regret marrying me, right?" His tone grew louder as many of our guests tried to avoid the awkward moment by turning away and pretending not to hear him. "I'm an embarrassment to you?"

"Of course not, Adam," I insisted. "Get dressed and let's talk about this in private."

"Let's not talk about it at all because I'm having fun with my friends." He began putting his clothes back on.

"Adam, pull yourself together, son," his father instructed with a firm stare.

"I'm fine."

"You're not fine!" His disappointed mother intervened.

"Okay, I get it," he said. "I'll calm down." I wanted to crawl into a hole and hide myself from everyone but, instead, I put on a strong front and pretended to laugh it off.

"Steve is over there talking to him," Delilah informed me. "It's all okay. He's just a little inebriated," she comforted. "We've all been there. Let's go enjoy your party."

I made my way over to our parents, apologetic and ashamed of his behavior. I felt sorry for them more than even myself because they had never before experienced that side of him. It had, up to that point, been hidden from them.

"I'm so sorry about this," I told them and they hugged me, assuring me that it wasn't my fault but, somehow, I still felt responsible. Adam kept his word, behaving himself for the rest of the evening.

"I'm sorry," he told me on the drive home. "I tried to make our anniversary special for you but I blew it." His words were still a bit slurred but he had, evidently, sobered up enough to realize his fault.

"I just really don't want to talk about it right now," I responded, knowing that a rational conversation probably wasn't possible with me angry and he intoxicated.

My disappointment would pass, just as it always did, and I felt guilty for ruining Adam's fun, even as extreme as it had become. His belligerence was no worse than anyone else's, I thought. Maybe I had let my fear of our parents' reactions spoil his night.

"Adam," I spoke softly as he drifted off to sleep, "I'm sorry, too."

CHAPTER 8

The next morning, I lay in bed, reflecting on the night before, with my husband next to me, still asleep. I struggled to look at him because of the anger and embarrassment that I still felt. He had branded both of us fools in front of our friends and family, and the images of it all were etched in my head. Once again, I found myself doubting the stability of our marriage and questioning how much longer we could survive its issues. Adam's most recent tour in Iraq had changed the person he was which, consequently, had also altered the way that I viewed him, and I feared that our family would never be the same. Needless to say, my husband awoke with a hangover, that morning, and the last thing that I was willing to do was cater to him.

"I'm picking up the kids and meeting my parents for lunch," I told him.

"Okay, babe," he replied, "but could you maybe get me a couple of aspirin before you go?" His impudence made me livid.

"You're on your own," I answered icily, closing the door behind me.

I dreaded the questions that I expected from my parents about Adam. In all of the years that we'd been married, they had never seen him in any way less than honorable, and I feared their reaction. I didn't want to have to explain his inexcusable behavior, especially in front of our children. We opted for a table outside, in the peaceful morning air.

"I can't get over how beautiful it is here," my mother remarked, inhaling the fresh Hawaiian air. "It's like being on vacation every single day."

"The air is always different when you're someplace else," my father chimed in. His feeble attempt at taking part in our conversation failed to mask what was really on his mind, and I wondered if I should say something about Adam before he did.

"What's good to eat here?" My mother, always the peacemaker, asked in deflection of the subject.

"I assume that Adam is sleeping it off this morning?" It was my father's first jab at his behavior the previous night. I saw my mother's elbow strike his arm, but it didn't deter his need for a response.

"I don't know what happened last night," I told them. "I guess he just had a little too much fun."

"You mean a *lot* too much."

"Hal," my mother scolded him.

"You're right, Dad. It was way too much." My words were like vinegar, admitting the obvious indiscretion of my husband, and it was I who bore the shame from my father. I felt like a child being scolded without warrant. I was being forced to swallow my pride while Adam endured no consequences, and it infuriated me. Admitting the truth was tempting so that the blame would live where it belonged, so that my parents could understand and, perhaps, sympathize with the situation. I wanted to express how Adam's last tour of duty had altered his character, and I wanted to describe to them his daily struggle to overcome what he had been through there. I yearned for advice from them, about our distressed marriage but, in the end, I didn't say any of it.

"Well, I hope it's a lesson learned," my father continued. "A man in his position has to carry himself a certain way."

"I know, Dad." The conversation had agitated me to the point of losing my temper, so I tried to change the subject. "How's your food?"

"Well, it's a little bitter," he replied, insinuating me.

"Yeah, mine too," I responded sarcastically.

"Sweetheart, we know that Adam is a good guy. He just had a bad night," my mother remarked. "It happens."

My father held his silence and I began to wonder if it was due to his own guilt from his younger bouts of drunkenness.

I returned home to find that Adam was gone, and a part of me was relieved. After the brash conversation with my father, I wasn't in the mood to see him. I was sure that he was with his parents, and I couldn't help but hope that he would stay gone for a while.

The silence sent my thoughts reeling about Adam and our marriage, not only from his actions the previous night, but for the weeks that he had been back home. Everything seemed to be spinning out of control, and my husband hadn't gotten the counseling that he had promised me he would. The sympathy that I had first felt for him had become frustration over the issues that he wouldn't fix. Heavy drinking was the only way that Adam could sleep through the night without an episode, but he couldn't continue using one problem to camouflage another. I felt guilty for all of the times that I grew bored with our normal, everyday routine because, at that point, I would have given anything to have it that way again. No one knew about Adam's drinking habit. I had become an expert at keeping it hidden, but that moment left me with a yearning for advice.

"Can you stop by?" I asked Delilah on the phone. She was the only person I felt that I could trust. We sat, in the consoling sun on my back deck that peeked out over Kanohe Bay, where I poured us some iced tea from a glass pitcher on the table.

"You look like you need more than that," my best friend commented. "Are you okay?" The tears that I had fought back all morning flowed, forcefully, down my cheeks, with no end in sight, as I finally broke down. They poured out my inhibitions and fear, my shame and my pride as I wept uncontrollably. Delilah hugged me, offering her stable shoulder to my weakness.

"What's wrong, honey?" She softly probed. I managed to pull myself together, and I began to confess the root of my anguish.

"It's my marriage," I told her, my voice crackling and shaken. After a deep breath, I told my friend how Adam had been changed by his last tour at war. I described to her, in detail, about his night terrors and flashbacks, as well as my fear of them, all which I had confided in her about before. "The problem is that, instead of getting help like he promised me that he would, he has developed a severe drinking problem to go with it." Delilah listened, intently and patiently, as I poured out my concerns, even studying my wounded eyes. I knew that she genuinely cared and wanted my marriage to work just as much as I did.

"I think that, sometimes, these guys view counseling as weakness," she said. "I mean, sure, we know it's a good thing, but it's not easy for the men to break down their barriers and ask for help. From day one of their military career, they're taught to be resilient. The military prepares them for war but not for its effects. Adam probably feels like numbing his feelings with alcohol is easier than asking for help." Delilah had shown me what I hadn't even given thought to, and I wondered if I hadn't empathized enough with my husband. Guilt punished me for focusing on my own feelings rather than his.

"I never even considered how hard it probably is for him to ask for help." The epiphany, somehow, eased my anger toward Adam, helping me to understand his reason for not getting the counseling he needed.

"He's a proud Marine, honey," she said. "Asking for help is like swallowing nails."

"Delilah, *you* should be a counselor."

"Should I charge you for this session?" It gave us both a chuckle, but her advice was, indeed, valuable to me, much more than she knew.

She left me in a different frame of mind, with more understanding of my husband and his needs. Delilah's words had, in a sense, strengthened my marriage, granting me the will and compassion needed to keep working on it. I only wished that I had solicited her advice sooner.

Adam walked in, and his nervous eyes met mine, still unsure what to say to each other.

"Where are the kids?" He asked timidly.

"They're in the backyard, playing," I answered, but it was obvious that there was more on his mind. "Did your lunch with your parents go okay?"

"Yeah. How about yours? Did you see them today?" The redundant small talk only got in the way of the conversation that really needed to occur between us.

"They made me realize what a jerk I was last night, and I'm truly sorry, Allison, because I wanted to make it a special night for you."

"It was special," I told him.

"I obviously can't keep going like this, drinking my nights away. You and the kids don't deserve it."

"I realized something, too," I said. "I didn't consider how hard it probably is for you to reach out for help. Delilah made me see that so I need to do more for you in that respect but, babe, even as tough as it is, you have to get the counseling that you need," I insisted. "I'll be right there to support you but it's time, now, to step up and do it. That's what the kids and I need from you."

Once again, he agreed to get help for his issues and to quit drinking. I wanted desperately to believe him and was hopeful of him following through, but doubt still nudged its way in. All I could do was hope for the best or prepare for separation.

Our parents were scheduled to fly out early the next morning, so we had them over for dinner that evening.

"It's been so nice being out here for a visit with you all," his mother remarked. "We've gotten to go sight-seeing, and we took walks on the beach. It's just been a wonderful trip."

"It sure has, for us, as well," my mother agreed.

"Well, we're so happy to have you here," I told them. "We wish you could stay longer."

"Yeah, us too, but Bud, across the street, needs my help building his shed," my father-in-law replied.

"It's more like he needs him to play golf," his wife joked, evoking our laughter.

"Come on out to Colorado so you can play a few rounds with us, son," his father urged. "Bud would love to see you again."

"Well, hopefully, we'll make it back there soon, Dad, but I have some things to take care of here first." We all understood that it meant getting the treatment he needed, and they smiled at him with gratitude.

"Maybe Andrew and Ana would like to visit this summer, when they are out of school, huh?" My mother suggested.

"Yeah!" Both of them cheered. "Will we fly there?" Andrew asked.

"Of course, you have to get over the ocean," she answered.

"Cool!" He exclaimed. The kids made a dash for their bedrooms after dinner, as they always did.

"Son, I'm proud of you for doing what is necessary for this family," Adam's father complimented. "It's not always easy to do what's right, but a real man will always put his best foot forward."

"Thanks, Dad. I will, and I just want to apologize to all of you, especially to my wife, for my actions last night. I was a belligerent fool who couldn't control his alcohol, and that's not who I want to be. Today, I'm clearly ashamed but ready to make a change. I give all of you that promise."

"I love you, honey," I said with a kiss, appreciative of his intentions.

CHAPTER 9

The week that ensued returned our lives to normal, with Adam working and the kids in school as I resumed my domestic responsibilities. Adam had already completed two therapy sessions for post traumatic stress disorder with a counselor, who prescribed him medications for anxiety and to help him sleep so that he didn't look to alcohol for it, and she would be working with him three times a week for intensive therapy. I was grateful for Adam's willingness to work through his issues, and I had high hopes for the future. Our marriage seemed to be healing as we spent more time together, just appreciating each other, and the romance that had been rediscovered. He and I made continuous efforts to flirt with one another, to hold hands or walk arm in arm, to gaze into each other's eyes in bed at night – all of the little gestures that are so easily lost in marriages. In ours, the spark that united us fifteen years prior had returned, and it was bliss.

Saturday was picture perfect under the sun and blue skies. I stood on the deck, preparing the grill for my marinated steaks while the kids frolicked gleefully in the backyard.

"Hey, hot mama," my frisky husband greeted from behind with his hands on my hips and a kiss on my neck.

"You're so bad," I giggled.

"You make me that way."

"Isn't the most beautiful day?" I commented.

"Yeah, it's… what is he doing?" His remark was interrupted by his sighting of Andrew, who was chasing his sister with a water gun. "What is he doing?" His voice grew louder and incensed. I hadn't had even a second to respond before Adam hurried off of the deck and into the grass. "Is that a gun?" I heard Adam interrogate our son as he snatched the toy from his hands. "You don't ever play with guns! Do you hear me, boy?" Andrew was distraught at his father's sudden outburst. We both were. Fear consumed his face as his father scolded him.

"Adam!" I intervened.

"There will be absolutely no guns in this house!" Adam yelled, and Andrew made a hasty retreat to his bedroom, clearly upset by Adam's explosion. It catapulted me into a rage, a mother bear protecting her cub and prepared to attack her enemy.

"What was that?" I probed furiously. "What the hell was that?"

"There will be no guns in this house!" He exclaimed. It was obvious that the toy had set him off, perhaps triggering something from the war. I didn't know what was going through his mind or what his issue with the gun was, but I refused to let him reprimand our son for it. I watched with dismay as my husband emerged with a hammer from the garage and destroyed his son's water gun, smashing it into pieces, and all I could do is shake my head in disgust.

"Do you feel better now?" I asked him with fury. "I hope you feel better now that you've just destroyed your son's toy and scared him half to death in the process." He glared at me with confusion as to why I was angry, as if I should have clearly understood and agreed with his actions. "You've got some serious issues that you better get control of quickly," I added, "because if you ever do anything like that again, the next thing being destroyed will be your happy home."

Andrew lay on his bed, sobbing, when I opened the door. His pain evoked mine.

"This isn't your fault, Andy," I assured him, sitting next to him on his bed, rubbing his back in consolation. "It's really not, and your dad didn't mean that." I took a deep breath. "The truth is, your father has seen some really awful things over in Iraq and, unfortunately, sometimes it really affects him more than we think it does. Your water gun is a good example of that." Of course, I had never told the kids about their father being captured in Iraq. "What he did was wrong, Andy. It was wrong and he knows it, but seeing it just triggered a horrible memory for him. It's not your fault, sweetheart. It's something that your dad is getting help for with the therapist." I hugged him as he calmed his tears and tried to rationalize his father's actions. It was then that Adam eased, empathetically in.

"I'm sorry, son," he said. "I didn't mean to yell at you like that because you didn't deserve it." Tears reappeared in Andrew's eyes as his father apologized. "You shouldn't be punished for my issues, and I'm sorry. I'm working with the counselor to fix them and be a better person for all of you."

"It's okay, Dad, I understand," our son replied, hugging his father.

"Babe, I'm sorry," Adam told me, outside of Andrew's bedroom, and forgiveness replaced my anger.

A couple of weeks later, Adam arrived home with a somber glare on his face, and I knew something was really bothering him.

"What's wrong? Are you okay?"

"Not really," he replied with his head hung in despair.

"Tough therapy session?" I asked. "You didn't get orders for another tour, did you?"

"No," he said. "Some things just came out in therapy, and the counselor thinks that you should do a couple of sessions with me."

"Me?" I thought. "Why me? Was I the reason for my husband's problems? Had I been one of his complaints?" Even if I was, I had to do everything I could to help him, so I agreed to go.

"Hello, Allison," the dark-haired, fifty-something therapist greeted with a handshake and a smile. "I'm so glad you could make it. Adam always has wonderful things to say about you."

"Not necessarily since I'm here," I thought, but what a relief it was to hear her words.

"He and I have been discussing some things that occurred in Iraq to cause his flashbacks and nightmares. I've explained to him that what he is going through is common for servicemen coming off of a tour of duty, due to the traumatic experiences that so many of them face, even on a daily basis. Through the process with Adam, he's been forced to relive many of his own experiences at war, which is very difficult for him. He has experienced some things there that you were never told about, at his request, and they have been weighing heavily on him. He's been wanting to talk about them with you but, because of its trauma to him, he has found it very problematic to do that. I thought that, perhaps, I could help him through it, and that's why we're here today." I had no idea what my husband felt that he couldn't tell me, and I was hurt by his inability to talk to me about it. Surely, we could work through whatever it was, I thought.

"I'm here for you, babe, no matter what," I told him. "I love you." I noticed his misty eyes before he dropped his head into his hands.

"After my capture, they um… I uh…"

"Go ahead, Adam," the therapist urged. Speaking is relieving, remember." He never lifted his head.

"I was tortured and uh…" He was battling through his statements, so scarred by his pain that he could hardly speak of it. I held his hands in mine. "There were others with me who were also tortured," he sniffled through his tears. We were kept in a stone room with no electricity and very little food. We were starved and beaten every day for weeks." He cried, his agony flowing through like fire searing his soul.

"Oh, honey, I'm so sorry," I said, holding him. The therapist explained that she had invited me to Adam's counseling sessions to hear what he had experienced in Iraq.

"It's so important that you know everything so that you can help your husband heal. You will be instrumental in his recovery," she said. "It won't all be accomplished today because it's too painful for Adam. We'll bring it out of him a little at a time. You see, Adam was the last one remaining when he was rescued," the therapist told me. I gazed at Adam, in awe of his heroics and strength for all that he'd been through. I was shocked by what I was hearing and had no idea that he had endured so much in Iraq. It brought much more understanding to his nightmares and his drinking. He self-medicated to escape the monsters that tormented his dreams each night.

"There's actually more to this story, Allison, and I have to warn you that it may be even more difficult to hear," the therapist told me. Part of me wondered how it could have even possibly been worse.

"It doesn't matter what it is," I assured my husband. "We'll work through it all together." He peered at me with his drenched, heartfelt eyes, and they spoke of something profound. I was growing apprehensive. He gently took my hands in his and began.

"I met a family while I was there, an Iraqi mother and her young son in a village that my unit was assigned to protect as part of our duty before my capture," he explained in a quiet tone with frequent glances at the gray carpeted floor. "I grew close to them, even treating the boy as my own because his father had been killed when he was four years old. His name was Azbar." The name rang familiar to me.

"Az, from your dream that night?" I queried. "I had asked you about it the next morning." He nodded. With tear-filled eyes, he looked into my eyes.

"He was killed. They killed an innocent little boy, and I had to look his mother in the eyes and tell her. It was the hardest thing I've ever done. She was inconsolable and so was I." Tears flooded his wounded eyes, and he took a deep breath. "We just grieved together and..." He was choked up and forced to muster up his courage while his entire body trembled. "We had an affair, Allison." His confession knocked the very breath out of me, like a swift punch to the gut, and I swore that my heart had dropped to my stomach while I hoped that I had heard him wrong. My face fell numb, and I felt like I would pass out. "I'm so incredibly sorry," he told me but it offered little comfort. "You have to believe, baby doll, that you're the one I love, and I never meant to hurt you." I couldn't even process his words at that moment. Out of all the horrible things that I expected to hear him say, an affair was the absolute last, and I was shell-shocked. I couldn't think. I couldn't breathe.

"It is important to know, Allison, that Adam's indiscretion, as wrong as it was, wasn't based on love," the therapist added. "He didn't love her. Often times, affairs are the result in situations of grief. They were both vulnerable and found consolation in one another. It's important to understand that it wasn't because of something you did or didn't do." I hardly heard her words from the shock that jolted and numbed me. All I could feel was betrayal and pain. My face seared with it. The world that I knew, the life that I knew, was crumbling around me and there was no understanding or forgiveness at that moment. All I could feel was the toxic blend of pain and fury, jealousy and insecurity, and I hated him for keeping the affair from me.

"I sat in that house, alone with the kids, all of us pining for you, praying for you, day after day, loving you and doting over you, even fearing for your life and, all the while, you were with another woman, another family," I seethed with anger. Never had I known fury the way that I did at that moment.

"It wasn't like that, Al" he tearfully pleaded.

"It was exactly like that!" I roared. "You found someone else to occupy your time with while your true family suffered. I don't care how you explain it away. That's what you did!" Adam hung his head, allowing me my feelings and realizing my right to them. "I was sad and lonely, so should I have had an affair, too?" I said with a steady flow of tears down my cheeks. "I didn't. All I've ever been is loyal!"

"Allison, your anger is warranted. What Adam did was wrong and unfair, both to you and to your children," the counselor said. "but after fifteen, otherwise, blissful years, I think that your marriage is worth saving, and I will ask you not to make any rash decisions that you could end up regretting later. Marriage counseling can help you work through it so that whatever choice you make is beneficial for the family." Her advice was sensible, but my wrath made me question if I even wanted to work on our marriage, if I cared enough to exert the effort to save it. I didn't know how I'd ever be able to trust my husband again.

"Do you love her?" I interrogated. I could accept a solely sexual affair over one where emotions were involved and romantic feelings had developed. It hurt to imagine him sharing his heart with another woman, the way that he did with me.

"No," he replied into my despairing eyes. "We just had this mutual grief between us. It was that we consoled each other. It wasn't about love, or even about sex. You have to know, Allison, that you're the only woman I've ever loved, and I never meant for this to happen."

"So, when were you going to tell me about it?" I interrogated. "You've just spent all of these weeks with me, happy and making love like it never happened. You never once brought it up, so when were you going to tell me?" My voice had grown louder with each word. I felt like I couldn't control the rage that I felt.

"I swear, I tried so many times, Al, but I just

couldn't. Look how happy we've been together. I just didn't want to ruin it." He seemed genuine and remorseful, but that couldn't mend my broken heart.

Halfheartedly, I agreed to go to marriage counseling with Adam, but it was exclusively for our children, who didn't deserve to suffer the consequences of our distressed marriage. I had no unrealistic expectations for the future, but I did want to exhaust every possible option before ever ending our marriage. I was a wretch, left broken and desolate as my world crumbled around me. Everything I had cherished about our marriage was gone in an instant. I tried to see his side of the situation but, in my mind, there was just no validation for being with another woman, no matter what the circumstances. It was bad enough that he had cheated but even worse was the fact that he hadn't told me about it. He had allowed me to continue believing in the sanctity of our marriage, that I was still the only one for him. I wasn't sure what the following weeks, or even months, would bring.

In the days that followed, my emotions remained a vicious combination of anger, pain and grief, and Adam and I would have to begin building our relationship all over again. Agony had stolen me, and I was unsure how to act or feel, uncertain of what to even say to him. I found myself wondering about the details of his affair with Ezra, the indecent things that were probably better left unsaid, like how often the two of them had been intimate and even if she was more satisfying in bed than I was. I simply couldn't understand how a person could be intimate with someone they weren't in love with. Part of me needed all of the private aspects but the other half of me thought better of it. The hardest thing of all was pretending, in front of the kids, that everything was normal between their father and me. I wasn't sure that it ever truly would be again. Adam seemed to be walking on eggshells, treading lightly and trying his best to restore my confidence.

"Allison, please, can we stop pretending that I'm not here, in front of you, and just talk about this?" He pleaded. "Please, I hate that you're hurting like this."

"It's a little late for that, don't you think?" I said. "Did you even consider the kids and me when you were with her?" I already knew the answer.

"I know how wrong I was, Al, but I need to make this right because I can't live my life without you."

"Well, I need you to give me some space for a while, okay?" The truth was, I couldn't even look at my husband, but worse was that I couldn't look at myself. What had he not been getting from me that made him seek out another woman? His affair brought out my deepest insecurities.

Adam was plagued with guilt and apologized a hundred times a day, but all of the I'm sorries were growing old. What I needed most was time. I hoped it would heal me and bring me to forgiveness. Always, I had sworn to never forgive infidelity. It was the one thing that I vowed would end my marriage, but I realized that it was much easier said than done. Maybe it was our kids who had changed my view but, whatever the reason, I was still there with Adam, hoping to fix it all. Still, I couldn't stand his touch, his hand on my shoulder, his lips on my cheek. It made my skin crawl, and I wondered how any counselor could possibly repair that.

CHAPTER 10

Our first couple sessions of marriage counseling were anguish for me, enticing me to give up. I felt humiliation and despair on that brown leather couch in the therapist's office, freely airing our dirty laundry to a stranger because we weren't capable of solving our problems on our own.

"I'm ashamed to be sitting here," I told the counselor through my flowing tears. I'm ashamed that I wasn't a good enough wife to keep my husband from straying. I feel like a doormat of a woman who would even try to forgive his betrayal without any real consequences. I just can't understand what made him want another woman."

"That's not who you are at all," the therapist reassured me. "You're a better person because you're willing to work on it and save your family. You see, this is not just about the two of you because you have children involved. A large part of this is for them." She fought to make me understand that Adam's affair had very little to do with me and that it wasn't my fault. She insisted that I hadn't done anything wrong, and she battled to take the blame from me, where I had a tight grip on it.

"This is all my fault." Adam accepted the blame, solely and whole-heartedly, never once tossing it to anyone else. "My wife is hurting because of me, even though she did nothing wrong," he told the therapist. "Allison, you're the best wife any man could ever have. Don't blame yourself for my mistake. I didn't search out another woman, and I never loved her. It just happened because we were both grieving, and that was wrong. Please, Allison, please believe that I never meant to hurt you. I guess I just needed the human touch, but I know how wrong it was. I swear, I've never, ever yearned for any woman but you." He accepted full responsibility for what he had done, but he didn't know how to make things right between us. Side by side on that couch, we cried together, the two of us tormented by the situation and the challenge to repair our marriage. At times, we wailed in desperation. I knew that he loved me and just wanted to fix it, but only time had any hope of healing me.

Adam and I gave our best attempts at pretending our marriage was still blissfully normal in front of our children, but I believe they saw straight through the mirage. Both had always been keen judges of character, and we weren't fooling them. They could see us acting just slightly differently than normal. They could see the change in the way that we looked at one another. They sensed that our chemistry was off. Their dubious stares lent suspicion, but neither questioned our actions. Because of what we were going through in our marriage, we were no longer sharing our bed. Either he slept on the couch or I did. I missed him. I missed the security and comfort of him holding me as I slept, but I couldn't seem to find forgiveness for his adultery.

Along with our marriage counseling, Adam and I continued his therapy for post-traumatic stress disorder each week. The road to his recovery was excruciating for him, forced to relive his nightmare in Iraq. The therapist prescribed him medication to help him sleep with Xanax to calm his anxiety, and they appeared to be helping.

The two of us sat in his therapy session, where the therapist asked him to recall the day of his capture. With a deep breath, he looked down to the floor, reluctant to revive the experience, and he took a slow, deep breath.

"They were disguised," he began. "Two of them had been aiding us for a several days, even feeding us information about key government targets. We were led to believe that they wanted to help the United States in our mission. One day, another Marine from our unit, named Chris, and myself went to meet with them in a house in the village." Adam dropped his head into his hands, covering his face. "We shouldn't have let our guard down like that," he said, regretfully. "We should have known better than to trust them. They and some other men took us, at gunpoint, into an abandoned building." It was clear that Adam was having trouble even talking about the events of that day as he clenched his jaw while tears welled in his wounded eyes. "There was no electricity and only a couple of small windows for light. There were other people there, chained to the wall in one of the rooms. I didn't recognize any of them but a couple appeared to be American. I think at least one was a journalist."

"What happened next?" The therapist asked. Adam sat, wringing his hands together as he spoke. He let out a sigh.

"They took me to another room and interrogated me about the goals and strategy of our military and our government. They made it clear that they despised Americans and wanted our military to leave their country. A man spoke a long dialogue about how Americans were shameful and arrogant and how our government was greedy. He seemed to just be expressing his point of view about us. I didn't say anything. I only listened while another man translated in broken English. After that, they chained me up with the others there while they interrogated Chris."

"What was going through your mind at that moment?" The therapist probed. He shook his head grievingly.

"What wasn't, you know? I had all kinds of thoughts racing through my head, like my family, my future, how long we would be there and what was going to happen to us. I really just assumed that they were holding us for some kind of ransom or something, for some kind of attention or reward from the United States. I knew that the military would hear about our capture and come get us, but it was waiting it out that we knew would be the true test."

"Can you tell me about the rest of that day, Adam?" The therapist asked. He talked about how he was left sitting on the floor and chained to the wall, and how he was fed only a handful of nuts with nothing to drink. He spoke of the other people there, who had also been captured. They looked bruised and exhausted, he said, but seeing American fighters had appeared to give them hope. Adam had told them to stay strong and not give up, and to trust in our military. "That night, right after I had finally drifted off to sleep, I heard a ruckus," he said and his face turned grim. "They were bringing in people from the village nearby. Azbar and his mother were two of them." I sat, in silence, listening to my husband speak about a world that was so foreign to me, and my heart was tormented as he talked about all that he had been through. I wondered how it was possible for him to switch between two countries that differed in so many ways. "They took Azbar somewhere separate from me, into another room. I don't think he knew that I was there. His mother was also taken to another room by two men and, a few minutes later, she…" He choked on his words and couldn't finish his sentence as he fought back the anger and tears invading him.

"It's okay, Adam," the therapist consoled. "Take your time." He took a deep breath and cleared his throat before continuing.

"Screams," he continued. "She was screaming. It echoed through the building, and I knew that Azbar heard her. Then, other women began screaming and crying. They were being raped and beaten, humiliated and tortured." Adam broke into tears and I joined him. "I tried with all I had to get out of those chains, even with that man pointing his gun at me. It went on for hours, and the sounds… I just couldn't stand the sounds." Even the therapist appeared sickened by the horror of his story. "They eventually let the women and the children go but kept the men there. We were starved, beaten and tortured almost constantly." He shook his head and stood. "I can't do this," he sobbed. "Can I have a minute?"

"Of course," the doctor answered and directed him to the restroom. I sat on that couch, just trying to wrap my head around what I had heard. It was difficult to hear it all, and I knew that living it had to have been complete agony for him and the other men. I was proud of him for finally getting it out. Several minutes later, he returned and sat back down.

"Sorry about that. I just… this is really…"

"I completely understand," she replied in her soft tone. "Are you okay to continue? I know how tough this is."

"Yeah, I think I can. It's hard, but I feel like getting it out is probably a good thing, right?"

"It absolutely is," she said. "Can you tell me what kind of things they did to you?" The therapist asked Adam.

"They broke a couple of my fingers, kicked and beat me until I bled, held my face in ice water, stabbed me a couple times." I hadn't had a clue about all that my husband had endured, and it suffocated me. It was then that I truly understood where his nightmares were coming from. "My treatment was mild compared to what some of the other men endured," he said. "A few of them, the American journalist, too, were beheaded right in front of me. They wanted to show me what was coming to me, and they wanted me to let the U.S. military know, too." With his head in his hands, he wailed like a child over what he had seen. "They always had blood on their swords. They thought nothing of taking lives, and worse was that they were doing it in the name of religion, but they thought the same about Americans. They were pissed about us killing their women and children, yet they were raping and beating them." Adam explained that, in Iraq, many of the women and children had been trained to kill Americans. It wasn't at all uncommon to be shot at by them or to have a grenade hurled at them. They had even seen female suicide bombers. "How do you help people that you don't even know you can trust?" He asked the therapist. "The woman you're trying to protect might pull out a grenade and blow you up. We just took our chances, day after day, minute after minute."

"Well, Adam, I certainly do applaud you for your courage and willingness to talk about this," the therapist said. "You've been through enough for today, so we'll continue next week?"

"Sounds good, doc," he replied. It took Adam several minutes to calm himself, and I walked over to him and put my hand on his back to console him. He peered up at me with flooded eyes and pulled me to him. I kneeled down to hold him, and it was the first time that I had touched him since finding out about his adultery. His arms felt like home while we both cried out our pain.

My husband did all that he could to mend our relationship. I could see his valiant efforts to earn my forgiveness and trust, but it was my own hurdles that refused to allow it more than that he didn't deserve it. I knew that forgiveness was imperative in order for our marriage to be repaired but I couldn't bring myself to return, or even receive, his hugs and kisses. The intimate touches that I once relished were what I feared the most. The only thing worse than his infidelity was figuring out how to forgive it. I just didn't know how and, at that moment, I wasn't ready to.

I tucked the kids into bed and returned to the living room where the flickers of candles danced, romantically, on the walls and a soft ballad whispered love into my ears. Adam walked slowly toward me, with adoration in his eyes and the irresistible smile on his face that I adored, holding out his hand for mine.

"May I have this dance?" He asked in his soft, deep tone. Flutters revisited my stomach, where they had made their home when we first met as teenagers, and I was mesmerized, drawn to him, yearning for the way that things used to be. My husband led me, gently, into his arms, the aroma of his cologne-accented skin intoxicating me with its pleasure. I loved him with everything that I had. My soul still craved him. Slowly, we danced, holding each other close and relishing the moment until I felt the burning of my dampening eyes. "I love you, my sweetheart," he spoke, with true sincerity, and I knew that he meant it. Gazing into my flooded eyes with soaked eyes of his own, he wiped away the tears. "I want you to feel it," he said, "this love between us. It's just you and me, babe, forever. I need you. You're my breath, and I can't survive without you." His words began to soothe my somber heart, and I depended on them. Adam's gaze fell to my lips, where his followed, and his velvet kiss sparked a thousand quivers down my spine. He kissed me softly and more passionately than had in years, and it was like falling in love all over again. His lips went in search of my neck but uneasiness invaded my bliss.

"Wait," I intervened, pulling slightly away. "I just can't. I'm sorry." Something in me refused his advances once again, and I was inundated with anger and guilt from it. Adam breathed a sigh of frustration, tossing his head back.

"I don't know what else I'm supposed to do here, Allison," he snipped. "I mean, I'm trying everything I know to make things better, but my wife won't even touch me anymore."

"Don't you dare turn this around on me!" I seethed at his audacity. Tears spewed from my scorned eyes. "You had sex with another woman! You shared what was supposed to be mine, ours, and you expect me to just get over it and move on. I can't do that, Adam."

"It didn't mean anything," he insisted. "It was sex, not love. We were just grieving and found comfort with each other but, I promise you, it wasn't love."

"It was more than sex. You shared your heart with her. You held her in your arms and kissed her, just like you do with me, so how is that not love? How does that not mean anything?" He hung his head in silence.

"It just isn't," I heard him utter as I retreated to our bedroom. My grief had become all too familiar as I lay, sobbing, on our bed. No matter how hard I tried, I couldn't rid myself of the vision in my head of them together.

"I'm sorry, sweetheart," Adam tearfully apologized, rubbing my back. "I'm just desperate to fix this because I don't want to lose you. This family is everything to me." I sat up and wiped my tears away, exhausted and sharing his need to mend the issue.

"What happened with her?" I probed of the details of his affair with Ezra.

"Allison, don't…"

"I need to know, Adam," I said. "I'm really trying to get through this, to forgive and trust you again, but I need to know about you and her."

"Please, you have to know how uncomfortable this is to talk about."

"Look, it's even more uncomfortable to me, but I have to know how far it went." I could see Adam's reluctance.

"It was just about grief, you know? It wasn't love. Azbar's father had been killed, so he always stayed close by me, more than the other kids there did. I think he looked up to me." Adam spoke of how he and the young boy became friends, talking and playing games, and teaching him how to be a man since he was the closest male figure in his life at that time. "Ezra was his mother who struggled, each day, without her husband. She appreciated my efforts with Azbar since he no longer had a father in his life." He described her as honest and hardworking, genuine and vulnerable, and I felt almost like I understood her. "You need to know, Allison, that there was never any attraction or connection between her and me during that time. It was nothing more than just a basic friendship, which I had with most of the people there. They just appreciated that we were there to protect them," he said. "After Azbar was killed and I escaped, I went to see her. Tears streamed from my husband's anguished eyes. "Neither she nor I intended for it to happen, Allison. I felt responsible for her son, and we were both just overcome with grief."

"But how did it turn intimate?"

"I don't even know, myself," he replied, wiping his face with his hands. "I held her one night as she cried, inconsolably, for Azbar, and she kissed me, mostly out of gratitude I think, because I was there for her. I was taken aback, and it was even kind of awkward, but I didn't stop her like I should have. I guess I was lonely and just needing something too, human companionship maybe. I don't know, but it just happened. I know I was wrong, Allison, and I should have stopped it."

"How many times? How long did it go on?" Maybe I was torturing myself with the information but part of me needed it in order to forgive him.

"Just that one time," he mumbled with shame, "and then I was sent back home. I think we both understood that it wasn't love, but just a sense of comfort. She knew about you and the kids." I was grateful that his story wasn't the sultry scene that I had imagined, and I even somehow sympathized with Ezra. Adam's version of events, somehow, lent a sense of understanding to the affair, even if I wasn't able to forgive it just yet. My husband's mistress, who I had pictured a sexy seductress, was just a mother, like myself, modest and grieving for the child that she loved.

"What does she look like?" I queried.

"It doesn't even matter."

"It does to me," I insisted.

Adam confessed that he had a single photo of the

Iraqi woman and her son and, hesitantly, he showed it to me. Tall and lean, Ezra stood, statuesque and innocently with a simple beauty, her long, dark hair draped, gracefully, over her shoulders. I could see why Adam was attracted to her. The young Azbar stood, obediently, next to his mother, her hand on his shoulder, with a faint smile of virtuousness that captured my heart. I analyzed the photo, the people in it not fitting their surroundings. The vision of the woman and her child made it difficult for me to be angry. My empathy tried to overpower the betrayal that I had been feeling. Seeing and learning about Ezra and Azbar somehow aided my compassion. I watched my husband look at the photo, carefully taking only a glance at it as not to anger me with a yearning of what he'd left behind in Iraq.

"What will happen to her?" I queried, extraordinarily concerned about her future.

"I don't know," he responded, brusquely, with uncertainty. Even in spite of my anger, I didn't wish any ill will on the woman. I was overwhelmed with compassion for her and the young boy. "My concern is you and this family, Allison," he reassured. "What I did was wrong, and I'm sorry. I love you. You're the only woman I've ever loved, and I just want everything to be normal again."

"I want that, too," I told him. "Just give me a little time to get there." I wanted, more than anything, to get back to where we were, when I could trust Adam and believe in him, but I didn't know how to, and I hoped that our counseling sessions would help us restore what was lost.

"Don't give up," Delilah advised when I confided in her about Adam's affair. "You have a solid marriage, and it's worth fighting for."

"I just feel so betrayed," I confessed. "I feel like it's my fault somehow, even though I know it really isn't. It makes me feel degraded."

"I know, but time will heal the wounds. Give your

marriage another chance. In fifteen years, this is Adam's only mistake." She was right, as usual. He had always been a model husband and father, never doing anything wrong before the affair. He was the kind of husband that all women wished for, kind and respectful, loving and genuine. Our marriage had always been strong, and it deserved to be revived, if at all possible.

CHAPTER 11

A couple of days later, the kids and I arrived home in the evening to find Adam sitting in the recliner, dazed and slurring his words. Fury consumed me as I glared at him in disbelief.

"Go to your rooms for a bit so that I can talk to your dad," I commanded Andrew and Anabel. I could feel myself inundated with anger that I couldn't control. "Are you drunk again, Adam?" I interrogated.

"No, nope," he responded in a barely audible voice. The television blared the commentaries of a panel of analysts debating their opinions and forecasts of the war.

"The reality is that we're spending far too much time and money on a war that we can't win," one voice spoke.

"So we're just supposed to sit back and do nothing until they bring their madness to our country? Our forces are overseas doing what they are trained to do, which is to defend against these terrorist attacks. We're sending a message here," another man rebutted. Adam shuddered as he watched, sweat beading from his flushed face.

"Bring our troops back home and let them protect our borders," the first man spoke again.

"What's going on with you?" I stared at him suspiciously as his head nodded in his battle to keep his eyes open and his reply to my question was no more than a mumble. "Why don't you go to bed," I suggested so that the kids didn't see their father in his stupor.

"Yeah." Adam stumbled his way out of the chair and down the hall, as if he was intoxicated, until he fell into bed. I shook my head in frustration but managed to carry on with my tasks.

"Why isn't Dad eating?" Andrew queried.

"He's just not feeling well tonight," I told him as the three of us sat down to eat, but I wondered if he really even bought my story. As much as I tried to mask the truth, I realized that the kids likely knew more than we thought. How could they not, I wondered.

"Tomorrow's our last day of school," Anabel cheered.

"Yeah! I'm so happy," Andrew added.

"Summer vacation," I said. "I know you're excited. You've earned it."

"I'm going to spend my whole summer swimming," my young son announced, and Anabel agreed.

"You guys are growing up way too fast!" I told them. "I'm proud of both of you."

"Are we going to Grandma's and Pappy's in Colorado?" Andrew asked. "They asked us to, remember?"

"Well then, maybe we can arrange a visit," I said.

The week that followed was more of the same with Adam. He lay around in a haze, his thoughts scattered and his words inaudible. He frequently repeated his statements and questions, as if he didn't recall prior conversations regarding them and he seemed to have lapses in his memory. Adam wasn't, at all, himself, and it was all too familiar.

"Here we go again," I thought. "This definitely won't fix our marriage." I went on the hunt for evidence, searching the house and trash cans for beer or liquor bottles. If he was drinking that much, there had to be some lying around, I thought, but I found none. He had been home on time every day so I knew that he wasn't someplace else drinking. His nightstand held the Xanax bottle. "It couldn't be," I thought, but I opened it to find it nearly empty. He had gone through the pills way faster than he should have. Abusing drugs was even worse than the alcohol, I thought, and I dropped to my knees with tears of desperation. "How do I help him?" I wondered. I couldn't take much more and, as selfish as it probably sounds, his illness was causing mine. I needed my husband back and, as much as I was trying to be sympathetic and understanding, my patience had found its end. I used the drive to Adam's therapy session to express to him how I felt.

"It's not a big deal, Allison," he said. "I just need them to deal with this shit right now."

"This isn't the answer, Adam." I needed him to find a better way to cope.

"She prescribed them to me for this reason, my anxiety," he argued.

"I understand, and I'm sure they do help when you're taking them the right way. You're taking two or three times the dosage."

"Look, you weren't there, okay? You didn't go through what I did, so I wouldn't expect you to understand," he snapped. "If I'm going to be forced to relive it all, then I need something to help me through that." There were so many more points I wanted to make, but the last thing I wanted to do was make him feel worse before his counseling session. I realized that it was better for me to try and be understanding at that moment. We sat in silence until finally pulling into the parking lot.

"How are you today, Adam?" The therapist greeted. "I'm alright," he responded.

I wanted to scream at her, chastise her for prescribing my husband the Xanax. I wanted her to know what it was doing to him and our family. It wasn't her fault though. Adam was the one who was abusing the medication, so only he was to blame.

After some small talk and a few routine questions, the therapist asked Adam to describe the day that he escaped from his capture. It was this leg of the story that was most difficult for him to talk about. He took a deep breath and began.

"Well, I had been there about three weeks and was

really worn down. I was filthy, frail from not eating and just beaten down and bruised. At that point, I had seen just about everyone else that had been there with us disappear. To this day, I don't know what happened to them. Only Chris, an Iraqi man and myself were left, but I could only think that we would be next. They had been threatening to kill us for weeks because we wouldn't cooperate with them. No matter what they did to me, I refused to give them anything they wanted. I figured by then that no one was coming for us. Maybe they thought we were already dead." He stared down at the floor. "I had begun to plan my death. I figured that, even if they didn't kill me, the beatings or starvation would. I had no energy left, no stamina, so I just started to accept those days as my last. I prayed a lot, asking God to forgive me for the things that I had been forced to do over there. I prayed for him to watch over my family." Tears drenched his eyes. "See, I wasn't afraid to die. That was easier than what I was going through, but I thought about my wife and kids every minute, every second, trying to remember if I had told them I loved them enough. I wasn't sure if they knew I had been captured, or if I was even still alive, and all I wanted was to tell them how much I loved them before I died. I worried about them missing me."

From the chair in the corner of the room, I broke down, hearing his words. Of all the things that must have been going through his head in captivity, my husband was worried about us, even more than himself. His words were gut-wrenching, and I could hardly stand to hear them.

"I thought about every single person that had ever been in my life, in one way or another, and if I had ever done anything that I needed to apologize for. I thought about the lives I had taken from families in the wars I had been in. That was the one thing I had always struggled with. We're trained to view them as evil but, in the end, aren't we all just people with different principles? God says that all people are created equal, so who was I to take another's life? I did it for my country. I took one life to protect another, you know? I lived my entire adult life according to the rules of the military, but I wondered if some of them coincided with God's laws. I really wrestled with that at the end." Adam spoke about all of the soul searching that he had done. "These things aren't easy to live with."

The therapist asked Adam to describe his escape.

"Well, that day, I felt that something was just different. I figured it was my day to die because we had refused to cooperate, and they had done all that they could really do to us, aside from killing us. I pleaded for them to let me meet my maker with dignity. I wanted them to allow me to wash up, and they agreed and released us from the chains. Outside, two men were standing with a boy. As I got closer to them, I could see that it was Azbar. They knew how close I had been to him. He had a..." Adam stammered his words and broke into tears. "He was wrapped in explosives and crying out to me."

"Oh, God," I whispered, not sure if I could bear to hear the rest of the story.

"I called out to him, telling him to be brave and that I would help him. I promised to help him!" He slammed his fist into the leather couch that we sat on, tears erupting from his eyes and his voice cracking. "I told the men to let him go and I would do whatever they wanted. Chris agreed. We were willing to do anything to save him. I pleaded with them to let him go. He was just a child." Adam cried inconsolably. "They made Chris and me get on our knees as they prepared to take our heads off, but Chris leapt up and darted toward Az." He wailed so much that he couldn't speak, and I moved closer and put my arms around him. I felt my shoulder soak from his tears. "They were both blown up in front of me." Silence encompassed the room. His words had left the therapist and me speechless. "I just ran and never looked back."

Adam had escaped the situation but not his nightmare. He would, forever, hold the visual of that explosion in his head. It was the root of his flashbacks and inability to cope back at home. It was what caused him to use alcohol and drugs as an escape from it. My heart ached for him, and I just wanted to help him.

I began to fall into my own depression, desperate for a solution to the issues in our relationship. My husband was broken. Our family was broken, and I felt like there was nothing that I could do about it. Therapy was our only hope. Adam had traded one addiction for another to flee from his torment and, though I understood why, I couldn't permit it. Every evening was an echo of the one before with Adam hardly able to function, and even the children caught on quickly, interrogating me about why their father was acting that way. I always blamed his "medicine" for his condition. After a few weeks, we were no longer even going to marriage counseling, and Adam's share of the household duties had fallen on me. I watched, with disdain, as my husband staggered clumsily around the house or slept every evening after work. It was as if he was numb to everything around him.

"Mom, are you still willing to take the kids for a couple of weeks?" I asked on the phone. They were better off in Colorado with my parents than at home dealing with the tribulations of their own, I thought. My goal was to get their father straightened out before they returned.

"Are you kidding? Of course I want my grandchildren!"

My next phone call was to his therapist.

"I would like to see about taking Adam off of this medication," I told her. "It's turning him into a zombie. He's really struggling to function." I didn't want to tell her that the real issue was my husband abusing it.

"The medication is designed to aid in his recovery,

if taken properly," she responded. "If Adam is abusing it then I agree that he needs to be weaned off of it. We can try some other ones that aren't habit-forming but I think that, given his sleep issues, it's necessary to supplement his counseling with some type of medication." It was almost as if she already knew what I refused to say, but I'm sure she had heard it all before.

The change in his prescription seemed to help. He began to behave like himself again almost immediately, to my relief, and I felt like everything would be okay after all. It was as if the world had been lifted from my shoulders, allowing me to breathe again, and I was so grateful. Adam didn't have any recollection of conversations and events that had occurred, other than regarding his work, which had been the only times he wasn't medicated. He hadn't even noticed the absence of our children right away. I was flabbergasted by the impact the medication had made, that it could alter his mind that much, and I was thankful that he was no longer taking it.

It was only a few days later that I found my hopes dashed, once again, when Adam's eyes admitted the symptoms of his old friend creeping back. I didn't need to investigate because the answer was clear.

"Why are you taking those again?" I hadn't even realized that there were any left in the house.

"I need them," he garbled.

"I thought you threw the rest of them out," I recalled, commencing my search for the pills. It was my punishment for trusting him to dispose of them. "You don't need these pills at 5:30 in the evening."

Frustration fueled my search as I checked in cabinets and drawers, in his pants pockets and shirts. We hadn't even repaired one issue in our marriage before another was created. Frustration had control of me, yet again, and I just felt like giving up. All I wanted was my husband back, and I didn't feel like it was too much to ask for. The war had taken him and given me back a man who could no longer cope coherently in the world. It was destroying our lives. I called Adam's therapist and told her about the medication.

"I'm searching but I can't find it, and he won't tell me where it is. I don't know what to do," I exclaimed, stripped of all of my dignity, wondering what she must have been thinking of us.

"Tell him that if he doesn't give you the medication, you will call the police," she advised peacefully, "and Allison, be firm here. Don't back down." When Adam still refused to cooperate, she instructed me to call the police.

"Are you serious? And tell them what?" Involving the police seemed excessive and absurd to me.

"Tell them your husband has illegal drugs in the house," she answered nonchalantly.

"They are drugs that you prescribed him!" I failed to understand her rationale, and there was no way that I would have my husband arrested and treated like a criminal on top of the issues that he already had. I felt like the therapist had instituted a problem that she wanted someone else to resolve, laying the blame on Adam for not being "normal" and, furthermore, an addict for being unable to cope in society without medication. Calling the police, for me, just wasn't an option. I wouldn't risk jeopardizing his career or further endangering his mental health. He was a wounded Marine, not a criminal.

I fell to the couch, in hopelessness, tears soaking my eyes as I buried my head in my hands. Adam hardly seemed affected, unemotional and dozing off in the recliner. I was the one suffering while he numbed himself to it all.

"I can't do this anymore," I surrendered. "I won't live my life this way." I felt like I had exhausted every option I had to help my husband. Nothing seemed to be working, and I didn't feel that the kids and I were even an important enough reason for him to stop the drugs. Xanax was the only thing that killed the pain for him. I continued to search the house until I found the few pills that were left and flushed them down the toilet. If he couldn't get access to them, he couldn't abuse them, I thought.

A couple hours later, Adam began to rouse from his nap and, after a quick trip to the bathroom, I watched him root around in his sock drawer for his pills. When he couldn't find them there, he searched his other drawers.

"Your medicine is out here, on the counter, babe," I told him, alluding to the new prescription that his therapist had given him.

"You know that's not what I'm looking for."

"Those are gone," I confessed. "I flushed them." Immediately, he was hurled into a panic.

"You did what?" He exclaimed. His face grew flushed.

"I'm sorry, sweetheart, but I did. You're not able to function with those, and I can't watch it anymore. Try the new ones that you were prescribed."

"They don't help me!"

"Hey, don't yell at me," I said. "You were abusing the Xanax. Even the kids noticed. Enough is enough."

"You didn't go through what I did so don't tell me what's enough!" He rebutted.

"You're right, Adam. I didn't go through that, and I'm so sorry that you did because it was awful, beyond awful but, babe, you can't keep doing this. We have a lot of issues in this marriage, and I'm willing to put the work in to fix them, but pills and alcohol aren't fixing anything."
Adam left the house, slamming the door behind him.

"Do you even care about our marriage?" I said while I followed behind him, onto the porch.

"Not right now," he replied as he got in the car and

drove off.

There seemed to be no end to my tears. Crying appeared to have become my new hobby. It was all that I had been doing and I found myself wondering if therapy was truly the answer. At that moment, I would have preferred to have lived in ignorance, not knowing the truth about Adam and his actions because, at least then, I was happy. My marriage was crumbling, my husband was crumbling. The war was tearing our family apart, and there didn't seem like I could do much about it. I loved Adam and our children more than life itself. Without them, I had nothing, but I owed myself more than what I was living. I wondered how much longer I could work on our relationship if he wasn't willing to.

It was late that night when Adam staggered through the front door. I had been snuggled up on the couch waiting for him and, once I knew that he was home safe, I retired to Anabel's room to sleep.

"Baby, come to bed with me," Adam pleaded, and I knew that he was drunk. "I'm sorry about earlier."

"We'll talk tomorrow," I said, wanting to avoid another argument.

"I love you, Allison. I'm trying so hard." No, he wasn't, I thought without answering him. "Come to bed so I can hold you tonight. Please, Al. Please."

"Go to bed, Adam," I told him, and he stumbled down the hallway. I had run out of tears and I was exhausted. All I wanted to do was get some rest and hope for something better the next day.

Early the next morning, the aroma of bacon and coffee tantalized my nose. The first thought in my head was the previous night and how Adam had said that he didn't care about our marriage. Our family was no longer a priority for him, and I was tired of waiting to be on his list of important things again. The self-medicating that he was doing had taken over his better judgment, and I felt that he needed to heal himself before he could even think of working on our marriage. I was selfish to want him to. In the kitchen, he cooked breakfast with a smile that hid the night's events.

"Good morning, gorgeous," he greeted me as if nothing had happened. "Want some breakfast?"

"No, thanks. I'm just going to grab a cup of coffee."

I felt him behind me, with his hands around my waist, as he gently kissed my neck. It felt so good and still so appalling, all at the same time. I edged away and out of his embrace, which clearly aggravated him, but I couldn't stand what was happening to us. Adam and I had always had the type of connection that other couples envied. We had never been so divided in all of our years together.

"What's a man to do when his wife won't let him even hold her?" He asked when he followed me to the deck. "How do we repair that, Allison?"

"I don't know," I responded, gazing out at the sun's tango on the water. "Sometimes I think I'm just in the way of you getting better."

"You're not. I need you, Allison. I need you to be my wife."

"And I need you to be the man I married," I turned around and told him. "I need you to be well again, without the drugs and alcohol."

"I don't know how anymore."

"Adam, I know how hard this is for you but we're just going in circles here. I get upset, you promise to stop drinking and then we're right back to it again," I sighed. "I don't blame you. You can't help what you were put through in Iraq. I'm to blame, too, for making it harder on you, but I don't know how to fix it."

"I don't either and it's killing me inside," he said, "but I have needs, too, and one of them is intimacy with my wife."

"I'm sorry but I just can't give you that right now."

Adam furiously left the house and returned that afternoon, drunk once again. He fell asleep in the recliner.

CHAPTER 12

As my husband snored, I crammed my clothes into suitcases, prepared to join my children and parents in Colorado. It wasn't at all what I wanted, but my own sanity demanded some time away. I realized that I couldn't fix Adam's troubles, no matter how much I wanted to. No one could help him if he wasn't willing to help himself. With desolation, I put down my suitcases and glanced around at what I was leaving behind, still hesitant to walk away. Each room and each piece of furniture held its own memory. I saw movie nights of popcorn and laughter on the couch and our kids taking their first steps down the hallway. I saw the kitchen filled with Christmas cookies and Thanksgiving dinner on the dining room table.

Adam was my life, and I wasn't sure how I would live without him or how we could be a family without him. He had always been the centerpiece of our family. I watched as he napped, free of his worries and the world around him. In the chair, he slept like a baby, sound and serene, oblivious to my tears and torment. I picked up my suitcases in my journey to face the world without him.

"Bye, babe," I whispered. "I hope you find peace."

I shut the door to my life, forced to begin a new one. The world seemed enormous and intimidating outside of the bubble that I had lived in for so many years, and I wondered what my future was. I had never been left to face it alone. Adam and I had always done it together. For several minutes, I stood on the front porch, petrified of the next step. I was safe where I stood, under the wing of my fearless husband, and treading on new and unfamiliar ground was perilous.

"I have to do this," I told myself. "Take the step and walk away." Rain poured down in a mimic of my emotions.

"Hi, doll," Delilah greeted when she drove up in front of the house. "Are you okay?"

"Not really," I confessed, fighting back the tears that threatened a return. My throat was pained from the lump in it.

"Come on," she consoled with her arm around my shoulder. "Let's get a cup of coffee." We loaded my suitcases and drove away as I watched my home gradually fade away.

"I just don't know what to do," I admitted to my friend.

"It's not an easy decision but only you can make it," she said. "Why don't you just stay with Steve and me for a bit? You don't have to leave the island."

"I know, and thank you," I replied, "but I really just want to be with the kids."

Delilah drove me to the airport where I boarded the plane to my new life. My hands trembled as my heart fought with my mind to stay.

"Am I really doing this?" I asked myself. "Am I just leaving everything that I know?" As the plane drifted down the runway, there was no turning back.

I gazed out the undersized window as we passed over land and sea, thinking of all the opportunity that it held. The kids and I could just start fresh, somewhere new, I thought as I tried desperately to convince myself that we would be fine. There were still a lot of things that I could do, I thought, aside from being a housewife. I had skills and talents that I could utilize in the world. I had chosen to stay home and take care of the children but I never had to. It was something that Adam and I had decided together when they were born. Still, I was confident that I could make it on my own. I had a teaching degree and had always wanted to get back into that.

Adam hadn't even been conscious enough to realize that I was gone, and I wondered if my absence would be enough to cure his addiction or if it would become just another excuse to feed it. I hoped he would put his family before the pills but I wasn't confident in it. I had completely lost faith in him.

What would I tell the kids, I wondered. I couldn't tell them the truth about their father and why I left. I wondered how our separation would affect them. They had parents who had always been together, blissfully together, and I wasn't sure that they would understand and accept anything different. Maybe they knew more than I was giving them credit for. It wasn't only me who had noticed the changes in Adam. They saw them too. The sudden ring of my cell phone invaded my thoughts.

"Hey, babe, where are you?" Adam asked, casually, evidently unaware of my missing belongings. He had probably just woken up, I thought, and assumed that I was merely out running errands or something.

"I'm on a plane," I uttered with uncertainty.

"What? A plane," he snickered as if it was a joke, "to where, Tahiti?"

"I'm on a flight to Colorado, Adam, and I hope you'll use our time apart to get well." Silence came over the line.

"Whoa, wait a minute," he finally stammered in a shaken voice, and I visualized him checking our bedroom for my clothes. "You left me?"

"I'm sorry. I just can't take it anymore. You need help, and I can't fix you, Adam. I knew you'd talk me out of it if I told you this morning."

"You left me for good, forever?" He attempted to comprehend my declaration.

"I hope it's not forever." I could feel my eyes stinging with the tears that threatened to return.

"Allison, don't do this," he pleaded. "I need you. I know I messed up babe, but I'll do anything to fix it, no matter what it is."

I smiled at his motivation but, in truth, I needed his

determination to be more than just a temporary thing to get me back. He needed to make a long-term commitment to himself.

"I need you to get well," I replied, "to stop masking your feelings and issues with the pills and be the man you were."

"I'll do whatever it takes, Allison. I promise."

"I hope so, and I'll just tell the kids that I decided to take a little vacation with them."

"Please, come back soon, baby doll," he spoke in a somber tone and it melted me.

"That depends on you."

I made it to Colorado, where my grinning father greeted me with a hug at the airport.

"How was your flight?" He asked as we retrieved my luggage.

"Not bad," I answered, "kind of therapeutic, actually." He set down the suitcases and put his hands on my shoulders.

"You stay as long as you want to, okay? Let Adam do what he has to do for himself." I had already made my parents aware of the situation between Adam and me, and it was their suggestion that I join them and the kids in Colorado.

"How are the kids? I can't wait to see them."

"They're doing great, and we've kept your visit a surprise, like you asked," he said. I was anxious to see them and hug them. I missed my children so much and hadn't seen them in two weeks. I wanted to focus on them and just relish our time together. "Look who I found!" My father announced at the front door.

"Mommy!" Anabel leaped into my arms.

"Mom!" Andrew joined in with a hug of his own.

"I missed you both so much," I told them, hardly able to let them go. It felt wonderful to hold them again.

"What are you doing here?" My son queried.

"Well, I missed you guys so much that I decided to take a little vacation with you."

"Where's Daddy?" Anabel asked.

"He had to stay at home and work, but he wants you to know how much he loves and misses you."

"How are you, sweetheart?" My mother asked when she hugged me.

"I'm okay, Mom," I assured her as well as myself.

After my long flight, I sat with my parents on their front porch while the kids ate breakfast. The fresh morning air of the Colorado mountains soothed me with its familiar scent, taking me back to my childhood, when I played in the yard and pretended that the screened back porch was my own house, where I was grown and married. I giggled at the memory, wishing that things were still that simple.

"I've always loved it here," I told my parents as memories of my childhood scrolled, like a photo album, through my mind. It was a different world than what I had grown accustomed to in Hawaii and, to me, it was unique from any other place in the world. I imagined myself living there again, the children and me, in a home of our own. It wasn't what I wanted, a life without Adam, but I needed to prepare myself for it in case he wasn't willing to get the help he needed.

"Are you doing okay, sweetheart?" My mother probed. I wanted to convince them that I was independent and strong enough to move on with my life without Adam in it, that I was resilient enough not to truly need him the way that I did. Maybe I was trying to convince myself of the same, but the reality was that I was dying inside.

"No," I admitted with a sigh, "but I need the peace of mind, away from him, right now."

"Adam just needs help," my father chimed in. "War changes a man."

"Your father and I can testify that even the tougher things can work themselves out if two people are willing to work on them. Our marriage has endured a lot of things and always prevailed, but it's never easy. It takes work," my mother said. I knew that my parents were right, and I hoped my own marriage would succeed, but only time could tell. "We're all happy that you're here," she added, "and your brother can't wait to see you."

My older brother, Mark, and I had always been close. We were only a year apart in age and, despite the occasional sibling rivalry growing up, we were friends with the same interests and hanging out in the same circle of people through the years. As adults, we remained close, talking on the phone at least once or twice a week. I hadn't told him about Adam and our situation, partly out of shame.

I was unpacking my suitcases when Adam called.

"I wanted to make sure you made it there okay," he said.

"I did," I replied. "Just got in a little while ago, actually."

"How are the kids? I'll bet they're happy to see you."

"Yeah, they're doing well. They asked why you didn't come with me. I told them you had to stay behind and work."

"I really miss you guys," Adam professed, and I missed him, too.

"I hope you'll get the help you need."

"I will, babe, because I want you all back," he vowed. "It's torture being away from you, but it has opened my eyes and let me know what I need to do. I want my family back."

It was unbearable being away from my husband and from my home. Living at my parents' house, in a bedroom, was an enormous change. I was surrounded by their things, rather than my own, and it made me uncomfortable. I wasn't sure what to do with myself, and I felt like an enormous burden. My parents suddenly had three more people in their house and, although they appeared to delight in having us there, I couldn't help but feel that they were laden.

Being back in my childhood home restored so many fantastic memories of growing up, like sleepovers with my friends in my lavender-accented bedroom and the tents that Mark and I constructed with blankets and chairs in the dining room. I recalled the heavenly aromas of my mother cooking in the kitchen while Dad reclined in his favorite chair, watching football on television. The home's walls still had the same floral wallpaper on them, and even much of the furniture remained the same. All that had really changed about my parents' house was Mark's and my bedrooms, which were now an office and guest bedroom.

"Hey, sis, are we all going out to dinner tonight?" Mark asked when he called.

"Yeah, if you're buying!" I joked.

"Deal," he replied. "See you in a bit."

We all met at a steakhouse, just a few miles away. The rustic log building looked the same as it had when Mark and I dined there with our parents as children. It lent a cozy feeling with its oak furniture and western décor. I had been watching the door, anxiously, until I saw Mark walk in. His dark hair and beard made him appear older than he was, but I knew those green eyes immediately.

"Hey, bro," I greeted with a hug, and he lifted me from my feet. "You look good."

"So do you," he responded. "It's been a while since I've seen you - too long." I hugged his wife, Andrea, and their two kids, all whom I adored. Andrea had become the sister I'd always wanted and our kids loved one another.

"Adam didn't come with you?" She asked.

"He had to stay behind and work," I fibbed for the sake of my children, but I felt as if she and Mark saw right through it.

"How long are you staying?" My brother queried.

"Um…" My parents and I exchanged a quick glance. "I'm not really sure yet," I stammered, "but at least a week or so." I wanted to confide in Mark about the situation with Adam and me but not in front of my kids. He glared at my distressed eyes with skepticism. My brother knew me, sometimes better than I knew myself. My parents had always said that we were like twins, him the male version of me.

"How about you and I go out for a drink after this, just catch up a little?" It was Mark's way of wanting to talk to me, alone. I was sure that he sensed the turmoil in my marriage.

After a leisurely dinner of conversation and laughter, my brother and I separated from the pack.

"Remember this place?"

"Sure I do," I replied with a giggle. "You and I spent some wild nights here with our friends, playing pool and getting drunk." The memories of us sneaking into the small bar with fake IDs came rushing back. I could almost see the group of us laughing and talking as the memories flowed through me. I reveled at how the establishment and its décor looked almost exactly the same as it had back then, with its scuffed wooden floors and dark walls. It was just a little hole in the wall kind of place that was always a ton of fun.

"Let's grab a beer," he suggested and we sat down at a small, corner table in the faint light.

"What ever happened to Casey?" I queried. He had been my boyfriend all through high school, the only guy I ever truly adored, up until Adam. Casey had broken my heart, and I had never completely gotten over him.

"He's still around. Never got married or had kids. He has his own business as an auto mechanic and he still plays the women." He always had been a bit of a ladies' man and that, in fact, was the source of our demise, when he cheated on me with my high school rival. "Every time I see him, he asks if you're divorced yet," Mark chuckled. "So, are you?"

"What?" His words left me flabbergasted.

"What?" He mocked in his best attempt at a female voice. "Come on, sis. Something is going on." I was always amazed at how well he knew me.

"You're right. Adam and I are kind of going through some things, a lot of things, actually." I confided in my sibling about all that had been plaguing my marriage.

"Wow, that's really tough, sis," he said. "I'm sorry to hear that."

"The kids think I'm just here on a mini vacation before taking them back home so, please, don't mention anything in front of them."

"Have you heard from Adam?"

"Yeah, and he's finally seeing how serious I am," I replied. "He's promising to get help now so we'll see."

The week at my parents' house felt like a year, each day slowly dragging. I used the time to visit old friends and enjoy some of the area's activities with the children. Adam called, faithfully, each morning and evening, to speak to the kids and me and with each conversation, his insistence that he was receiving the help that he needed.

"Please, come back home," he often pleaded. "I need you and the kids. I miss you guys so much."

I was always so tempted by Adam's words. There was no place I wanted to be more than back at home with my husband, but I had resisted his persuasion. As much as I yearned to be with him, I wanted to be sure that he had regained control of himself before I returned with our children.

Friday night led me back to the bar, where I had been invited by a few of my old high school friends. In my floral sundress and sandals, I walked in to find the group already there, along with my brother and sister-in-law.

"There she is," one of them announced.

"Hey, sis!" My brother greeted with a hug. I ordered a beer and was socializing when Mark nudged me on the arm. "Look who just walked in," he said. I turned to see Casey walking up to the dark oak bar. "your ex," he added with a snicker.

A flutter stalled my heart when I spotted my former high school flame, still handsome with his sandy blond, layered hair, draped across his shirt collar, and his bronzed, muscular physique. I fought to keep my curious eyes from scanning the back of his faded jeans as he joked with the bartender. The eyes of my friends studied me with the recollection of how inseparable Casey and I had been during our high school years. I forced my gaze from my former flame, pretending that his presence didn't affect me though, in truth, his being there had captured every ounce of my attention. My heart raced as I struggled to ignore Casey while proving to my friends that I no longer had feelings for him.

"Al, did you see who's here?" My friend asked me.

"Yeah, I saw," I answered, casually, as if it didn't matter. I felt like a teenager again, standing with my friends and trying to earn the attention of a cute boy, and I almost had to remind myself that I was grown and married. Still, I couldn't deny that I wanted Casey to notice me. I wondered if the chemistry, once so powerful, between us remained. It wasn't that I wanted to cheat on my husband, or even thought about it, but there was no doubt that I hoped he was still attracted to me. There was no reason for it, other than to feed my ego, but it was innocent, I felt. It was almost as if everyone was waiting for Casey to approach me and, even though I hoped he would, their gawking was awkward.

From the corner of my eye, I saw Casey turn away from the bar and take notice of us, and then of me. I stood out to him, among the crowd, just as I'd hoped I would. He observed me, for several minutes, in intense observation, like he was making sure it was truly me that he saw, before walking toward me. I could hardly breathe from my anxiety of his approach but it seemed silly. I was married and long over Casey.

"Well, look who it is," he greeted with the toothy grin that I remembered so vividly. "How have you been?" He pulled me close to him for a hug and, even after so many years, it felt wonderful, his brawny arms cradling me, securely, to his chest. I found myself intoxicated by his aroma as I breathed him in deeply.

"I've been great," I responded with a bashful smile. "How about you?"

"I can't complain," he answered. "You still hanging out in Hawaii with that husband of yours?"

"Yeah, for about fifteen years now," I uttered. "He had to stay back there and work while I'm out here visiting."

"Oh, well, that's too bad," Casey joked, flirtatiously, and I remembered how my brother had referred to him as a lady's man. I wasn't about to be his next conquest.

"I heard you're in business for yourself," I remarked to change the subject. I have to admit that I didn't hear a single word that he spoke on the subject. I gazed at him, like the teenage girl that used to admire him, mesmerized by his hazel eyes and succulent, alluring lips. He was even more attractive than all of those years ago, and my mind wandered back to our intimate moments. My lips craved his as our eyes were entranced. My heart raced with stimulation as I thought about what it would be like to make love to Casey again.

"What are we talking about over here?" My nosy brother had interrupted my incredible fantasy.

"Just catching up," I replied with the false smile that replaced my frustration.

"I tell Mark, all the time, that I'm waiting for you to

get divorced," my former boyfriend joked, and Mark and I glanced at each other, thinking "if he only knew."

"You haven't changed at all," I ribbed.

"We had some amazing times," he recalled.

"Yes, we did, especially here, in this place."

The bar, in our high school days, was the site of many cherished memories with our friends, and the three of us reminisced about them, laughing at our antics back then. Adam had come along after that and had never been there. My life before him had been so different, and I think that even I was different back then, a careless teenager, so free from the concerns of the real world. I felt invincible then. It was the best time of my life. Adam hadn't taken that away. Age had. Having children had, but I wouldn't have traded my life with Adam and the kids for my carefree days, not for anything in the world. My family was my everything.

"I'd love to take you to dinner while you're in town," Casey said, but I was hesitant. He and I, alone together, was lethal to my already wounded marriage. "I see the caution in your eyes, but it will be completely innocent. I promise. I respect that you're married."

That night, as I lay in bed, tender memories of Casey revisited me. Years had gone by since I had last thought of him, but our reunion that evening had brought back all of our good times together, all of the attributes that made me fall in love with him back then. I recalled the beginning of our relationship and the exhilaration that it lent, when he and I did whatever it took to spend time together, times alone that we spent kissing for nearly an hour straight. I still saw his gaze into my eyes, that moment of realization that he loved me. Casey and my relationship held many facets of romance. We had dined by candlelight on the dinners that he cooked, and I remembered him carving our names in a tree during one of our quiet walks. Once, he had even walked across town in a snowstorm, just to see me. The memories streamed in, making out in the backseat of his car parked by the river at night, the windows inundated by the frosty night's fog that glistened in the moonlight while our body heat kept us warm. I had suppressed the memories since I had met my husband and, until that night, forgotten a lot of them. Though it should have been Adam who occupied my thoughts, Casey took his place until I drifted off to sleep.

CHAPTER 13

The next morning, I was awakened by the ring of my cell phone and, for a single moment, I hoped it was Casey.

"Hello," I answered.

"Good morning, baby doll," I heard Adam say, and it made me smile.

"Hi, babe. How are you?"

"I'm doing good but missing you and the kids." His tone was grievous and dismal.

"I miss you, too," I told him, and I meant it. Casey had been in my head but my husband remained my priority. "So do the kids."

"How are they?" I told him how much fun they were having and how spoiled they were by his and my parents. I had hardly seen them between their time with each of our families. "I've been making real progress with my therapy," Adam boasted, and I was proud of his success.

"That's so great, babe!"

"I hope that means that you'll be back soon," he said. "I really miss you, so much. I want to hold you again, Allison."

I wanted it, too. There was nothing I wanted more than to go home to him. I didn't want to burden my parents any longer and, as much as I loved them, I just needed my husband. I missed his presence, and my heart ached for him. I craved his smile, his kiss, his touch. I missed my home and my family. After nearly two weeks in Colorado, I booked the flight for the kids and me to return to Hawaii.

"Are you sure this is what you want?" My mother asked me. "You can stay here as long as you want to."

"I know, Mom, thanks. I just feel like it's time to go back home. I miss my husband, and I know the kids are missing him, too." She saw the anguish in my eyes and sensed the yearning in my voice, and she understood a woman's need for her husband. Even with as much as the children were having, they were eager to get back to our home in Oahu, as well.

"We're coming home tomorrow," I told Adam on the phone, and he was thrilled.

"Everything is going to be perfect for you and the kids, Al," he vowed with anticipation of our return. "I'm so happy you're coming home, and I can't wait to see you guys."

That evening was my scheduled dinner with Casey, and I called him to cancel our plans. Too many emotions had returned so I felt it best to just walk away quickly.

"Aw, come on, Allison, don't cancel on me. I've already made the reservation," he said.

"I'm sorry, Casey, but I…"

"Listen, I told you, it's just an innocent dinner between friends, in public, where nothing can happen. We go way back, so let's just have a nice dinner before you leave tomorrow." He was right, I thought, and I was making a big deal out of nothing. I was letting my feelings dictate the status of my friendship with him when, in reality, he probably didn't even feel the same way, so I had no valid reason to be concerned. My own ego had gotten the best of me.

I put on a navy sundress and sandals, careful not to appear too alluring. My apprehension grew more prevalent in my battle to stay calm. Part of me wished that I had never agreed to have dinner with Casey, but I couldn't deny the other part of me that was eager to spend time with him again. Already, it felt wrong, like I was betraying my husband.

"It's innocent," my mind replayed Casey's words, and it, somehow, eased my angst.

I walked into the intimate, amorous setting at the

restaurant of faint lighting and soft music. Only a few tables could accommodate more than two guests, and I noticed that all of its patrons were couples. I was struck with unease, having expected a less formal atmosphere.

"Right this way," the host greeted, leading me into a small, more private room of only a handful of tables.

Adam rose from his chair with a single red rose and a pleased smile and, immediately, everything that I'd always felt for him came rushing back. My stomach could hardly stand its fluttering as I tried to steady my breathing.

"What did I get myself into?" I thought at the tantalizing sight of him in his navy suit. "I'll bet he smells as good as he looks."

"Hey, glad you could make it," Casey greeted with a hug, and I was right about his scent. He had always been impossible for me to resist, and it was obvious that nothing had changed. "You look amazing."

"Thank you," I replied, though I felt underdressed for such a formal establishment.

"I hope you don't mind. I've already ordered the wine – Pinot, if I remember correctly." I was impressed. "I'd like to propose a toast," he said, "to old friends."

"To old friends", I echoed, lifting my glass to his. "I'm so glad you came out with me this evening, Allison, especially since you're leaving tomorrow."

"Well, I have to confess that I was hesitant."

"I know you were and, believe it or not, so was I," he responded. "Seeing you again definitely stirred up some old feelings, even some that I thought were long gone." I knew exactly how he felt. "I hope your husband won't mind us being out together because I really do have good intentions."

"I'm sure that he's completely fine with it," I answered, though I didn't have much confidence in my statement.

"He's a very lucky man."

"How come you never settled down and got married?" I probed. A man as attractive as Casey was never single for very long.

"Still haven't found the right woman, I guess," he responded, "but being single is a lonely life, sometimes. I'd like to settle down with a good woman."

"Well, I hear you've been through a few hundred already," I ribbed with a hint of curiosity.

"Real funny!" He grinned. "I just haven't found any that compare…" Casey forced a halt to his sentence but I knew that 'to you' were the words he didn't say. I wasn't sure if he meant it but it didn't matter anyway.

"I just haven't found the right chemistry with any of them," he corrected, peering down at the table. "You sure bounced back quickly though!" He joked.

"Well, I don't know that it was exactly quickly," I rebutted. "It was brutal getting over you. I was heartbroken for a long time."

"Oh, come on. I doubt that."

"It's true," I insisted. He stared into my eyes as if caught off guard.

"I didn't know that," he finally uttered, seemingly ridden with guilt. "I mean, I didn't realize…"

"It's okay," I intervened. "It all ended the way that it was meant to."

"I'm sorry, Allison," he said, "for hurting you like that, and for everything else I did. I was young and dumb, and I didn't know what I had until it was gone."

Our conversation had turned personal, almost immediately, despite our intentions of keeping it lighthearted, but his words were a ballad in my ears. Finally, he had set his ego aside to apologize for the way that he had treated me. It was all I had ever wanted from him.

"Believe it or not, I do regret it because you're the one that got away." Casey spoke with more sincerity than I had ever heard from him, and I was the blushing school girl that I used to be. His infidelity, back then, had destroyed me and, in my own mind, lessened my value to him. It had stung me with the feeling that he could easily move on without ever looking back at me. My plan had been to break off our relationship until Casey earned back my trust. In reality, he gave up before I could even accept his apology, and both of us moved on, never reconciling at all.

"Oh, come on," I rebutted.

"I have dated a lot of women. That's true," he continued, "but it's only because I can't seem to find my type. My friends call me picky but, the truth is, I'm looking for that chemistry, you know, like you and I had. I just haven't found it."

"I think that love comes with many faces," I responded. "I mean, I'll admit that we had a chemistry that I haven't found again either, not even with my husband, but he and I have a different kind of love and chemistry that's just as good."

"Adam is a very lucky man. I hope that he appreciates you like you deserve," Casey remarked. "I can't deny that I wish it was me. It should have been me in his shoes."

"That means a lot to me. Thank you." I was left with little else to say. His sentiments had astounded me and, for only a second, I wondered if knowing his feelings, back then, would have made a difference in our lives.

After filet mignon and two glasses of wine, Casey walked me to the car.

"Thanks for dinner," I told him, struggling to turn away from his gaze that always left me mesmerized.

"I hope it won't be twenty more years before we see each other again," he said as I opened the car door.

"I hope not either." I hugged him, and he placed his hands on my cheeks, looking into my eyes. My heart raced in anticipation of what would happen next but I couldn't stop him, even as much as I knew that I should have. I wanted to feel his lips on mine one more time, and I felt indulgence before we even touched. His warm, soft kiss thrilled me with its fulfillment, and I melted into his arms. We kissed long and slowly, his lips meshed passionately with mine in bliss. I had craved that moment so many times after our relationship ended, even during the beginning of my relationship with Adam. Just one more kiss. It felt natural, even all of those years later.

His lips left mine, with unwillingness, and he gazed lovingly into my eyes. My chest ached from my pounding heart, the yearning of him, and I saw the same in his breathing. Casey brought his lips back to mine, pressing me against the car with his body. The ecstasy that I felt was overpowering, and I wanted more of him.

"God, I've missed you so much, Allison," he said and then kissed me a third time, even more avidly, as if I was nourishing something inside of him. At that moment, we needed each other, desperately, unable to let go of each other. We hungered for one another, starved for the affection. It had been so long since I had felt his arms around me, and they felt safe.

"I need you again." The words had been spoken before I could even think, but I meant them. I yearned to make love to Casey again, even though it was wrong. I was helpless to stop it. Maybe I just didn't want to stop it. I was doing the same thing that Adam had done to me, but I couldn't pull myself off of my temptation.

"Are you sure?" He asked. I was acting in the heat of the moment which, even as much as he wanted me, too, he wouldn't take advantage of unless I truly meant it. For a few seconds, we broke apart to cool off and think rationally. I wasn't doing it because my husband had, or because I wanted to pursue a relationship with my former lover. I simply craved him. I was well aware of the risk, but the reward seemed to outweigh it.

Rain speckled the windshield of my father's car as I followed Casey down the dark and desolate road to his house, just outside of town. My mind raced with thoughts of Adam and how what I was about to do could affect our marriage. It wasn't revenge for his affair with Ezra, but I have to admit that it did lessen my guilt.

"I should just turn the car around and forget about this," I thought. Two wrongs didn't make a right, and Casey would certainly understand but, in all honesty, I wanted to make love to my former flame again. I yearned for his touch one final time.

The two of us ran out of the rain that poured, to the covered front porch of his restored, older house. I remembered it from my childhood, where he had lived with his parents.

"I can't believe you still have this place," I commented.

"My parents left it to me when they died, so I fixed it up a little." He opened the door to a spacious living room of polished wood floors and walls of vivid hues, accented with western décor. The extraordinary fireplace that served as the room's centerpiece had been refurbished with new brick, and a substantial bear skin rug lay in front of it.

"Casey, this is stunning," I complimented. "I had no idea that you were this talented." It didn't look like the bachelor pad that I had expected it to be, and I was immensely impressed.

"Thanks," he replied proudly. "I refinished the whole house."

He led me through the oversized kitchen of gorgeous oak cabinets and iridescent granite countertops, the dining room and study, also refinished with oak, and then to his captivating bedroom of red walls and black lacquer furniture, where I envisioned his many trysts.

"I brought you in here to show you the other fireplace that I built," he grinned, diverting my attention away from the obvious. "Let's get a glass of wine."

Roaring thunder and lightning accompanied the downpour outside as I sat on the couch, peering around at my immaculate surroundings. Guilt assaulted me for feeling so comfortable there. It was a place that I could easily imagine myself living in with Casey and my children, but I knew that it was appalling for me to be thinking it. I belonged with my husband and where I intended to be. I knew that Casey could never give me what Adam did. He wasn't the family man that I needed. His entire lifestyle was different than mine and he didn't fit into my world. Still, the moment had united us and, tomorrow, I would tell him goodbye.

"For you," Casey said, handing me the glass. He sat next to me on the couch. "What should we toast to?"

"How about a fantastic night of lasting memories?"

"Sounds good," he responded and we lifted our glasses.

"This really is a great house," I complimented.

"It's missing a woman's touch," he sighed, "someone like you, a woman who can fill it with love, you know?" I nodded in understanding of his sentiments. "People joke about me dating different women, like I'm a playboy or something, but that's not me at all. I'm looking for the right woman. You're her, Allison. No woman has ever compared to you, and it's you who belongs here, you and your kids."

Casey's words were heartfelt and sincere, and I sat, with flattery, listening to him dote on me that way, but I wondered how much of it was authentic. I had waited many years for those words.

"Why now?" I asked him. "Why didn't you say all of this then, when our relationship was ending and I cried for you, pined for you?"

"I told you, I was young and dumb, arrogant in thinking that I needed other women while I let the only one who really mattered slip away. It was the biggest mistake of my life. I'd give anything to be in your husband's shoes, holding you every night and seeing you next to me each morning. I hope that he appreciates you."

The truth is that I didn't feel appreciated by Adam. I wanted him to feel what Casey did but, instead, we struggled to stay together. Why didn't it flow easily for Adam and me the way that it did for Casey and me? I still fought to forgive my husband for his affair, and his focus was coping in civilian life.

In front of me sat the only other man I had ever loved. There was a time when I loved Casey even more than life, and it was always so easy for us. We never had to make any effort to stay together. The chemistry between us had always been fiery and natural. It still was as I gazed at the man who had been such a huge part of my life all those years ago. I feared losing him again, but it was inevitable because I'd chosen to make my life in Kaneohe Bay with Adam and our children.

For the moment, though, I was with Casey. It was just the two of us and all of the feelings that we'd left behind. They stirred erratically inside of me, thrilling me with the possibilities.

Slowly, I returned my lips to his, uniting them again in zealous motion. His kiss set my very soul ablaze, and I craved all of him. He held my face in his hands as I climbed, seductively, onto his lap, straddling to face him. His hands moved to my back, pulling me closer to him as my heart pounded against his. His satin lips traced my neck and lobe, his stimulating moan adding to my exhilaration. I grasped the back of the couch, behind his shoulders, as I felt his bulge through the thin polyester of his pants, pleading for me.

"God, I need you so much, Allison," he whimpered in his deep, inviting tone.

"I need you, too."

Slowly, he pulled my dress up, over my head, removing the obstacle before him, along with the lace bra that battled to hold my breasts hostage. He cupped them gently, in his enormous hands, as my matching panties danced against his manhood until I felt like I would explode. I removed myself from his firmness and unbuttoned his pants. He lifted his hips for me to pull them off while removing his shirt to reveal defined abs. Casey descended onto the floor, leading me to the bearskin rug, where we freed ourselves of our remaining clothes. He spread me out before him, a buffet for his sampling, and his lips began their erotic exploration from my neck to my breasts then, gradually, downward to my stomach and legs, leaving the best for last. His trek was leisurely and tender, unhurried in adventure, which only added to the thrill. I tingled with anticipation as he teased around the sweet spot until, finally, the faint tickle of his tongue that only barely scathed me. I let out a moan and a series of whimpers as the pleasure of his strokes enveloped me. My hips were lifted from the rug by his robust hands and delivered to his mouth, where a great symphony was played on me. I bellowed with gratification as Casey emitted orgasmic shudders through my body.

"You taste so good," he whispered and, in a single, miraculous movement, swooped me onto his face as he lay on his back. His tantalizing dance continued, delighting me so unselfishly, and I felt guilty for not returning the same to him, but it was reserved for my husband. I positioned myself onto his throbbing muscle, which evoked simultaneous groans from both of us. We began a slow rhythm that I feared would force a premature finish from him.

"Oh, God," he moaned with his eyes closed in ecstasy. Our bodies danced a slow and erotic pace with one another, each savoring the bliss of the other. "You feel so good," he whimpered and, though I uttered not a single word, his remarks threatened my explosion. He raised his hips, creating a mound of pleasure for my amusement, and I yelled out with pleasure as I grinded into intense waves of orgasmic delight, my entire body quaking uncontrollably.

He had propelled me into another universe, twice over, and I was thrilled with his longevity as he gently lay me down on my back and reentered me with a little more aggression. He gyrated with gentle teasing, held above me on his sculpted, trembling arms.

"Mmm, I can't take it anymore," he whined and extended my knees to my head before thrusting firmly into me a few times and crying out with satisfaction as I quickly followed. We lay together, sweating and catching our breath.

"Wow! That was incredible," Casey complimented, and I agreed, but the guilt intruded without hesitation.

I couldn't believe that I had just been unfaithful to my husband, and I was immediately consumed with shame. He didn't deserve what I had done and I felt filthy, appalled by my behavior. Suddenly, my nudity embarrassed me. I was discomforted by Casey seeing my bare body because only Adam was meant to look at it. I scurried to the bathroom, bashfully holding my clothes in front of me.

"How could I do that?" I interrogated myself in the mirror over the sink. "How could I be so heartless and stupid?" Regret, like I'd never known, had taken me over, and all I wanted to do was leave. I freshened up and returned to the living room, where Casey wore nothing but a smile.

"Already dressed," he observed. "If I didn't know better, I'd think you're trying to rush out on me." He made his way to the bathroom as he spoke. "Was I that bad?"

"No, no, of course not." He was actually quite phenomenal. "I just…"

"What?" He asked, reappearing with a towel loosely draped around his hips. "Oh, I see, your husband, right?" I nodded with guilt.

"Yeah. I'm sorry, Casey. I mean, I wanted to do it, and it was incredible. It's just that, well, I just..."

"Feel a little guilty?"

"A lot, actually," I replied. I felt like a school girl, reckless with my decisions.

"Listen," he said with his hands on my cheeks, forcing my pitiful eyes to his, "I understand how you feel. We acted on some old feelings that were brought back, and you have a family with him. But I want you to know that I did it out of love, not to use you or anything. I respect your life with him, but I don't regret what just happened. I'll always have love for you, no matter what, but this will stay between us."

"I guess I got caught up in feelings that I didn't even realize were still there."

"I'll say, again and again, that I wish it was me in Adam's shoes, so I hope that he appreciates you."

"Thank you, Casey," I replied. "That means a lot to me." I told him goodbye and returned to my parents' house to pack for the kids and me. There was nothing I wanted more than to go back to Adam in Hawaii.

CHAPTER 14

The night's silence enveloped me as my father drove the children and me to the airport. It was 3 a.m., and the kids resumed their sleep in the backseat.

"You're doing the right thing, sweetheart," my father remarked as if he could read my mind. "Those kids need both of you."

"I know. I just hope that Adam is still getting the help that he needs like he says he is."

"Well, then, I think you've got to give him a chance to prove it," he told me, "and if he doesn't, then you know that your mother and I are here to help with whatever you need."

"I know, Dad. Thanks."

At the airport, the kids and I bid our farewell to him and to the Colorado peaks.

"Take care, kiddo. I love you." My father squeezed us tightly and watched as we boarded the plane.

The long flight lent hours for me to think about what had happened with Casey and what my future was with Adam. My once perfect life had become chaos, and I didn't even know how it had gotten to that point. All I wanted was what used to be with my family, our secure life together. I craved the normalcy that once was, and I was willing to do anything to get it back. I thought back to the beginning of my relationship with Adam and how we had fallen in love almost immediately, something so blissfully unexpected in the wake of Casey, who had left me so heartbroken and unsure of myself. Adam had stepped in and picked up the pieces. He reestablished my value and had proven himself ten times the man that Casey was. Never once had I regretted marrying him, and being his wife granted me pride.

I was wrapped in guilt for my fling with Casey because Adam didn't deserve it, and Casey didn't deserve me. I regretted acting so hastily on the feelings that I had that night and wished I'd never seen my former boyfriend at all during my visit. Still, I couldn't take it back. The only way, I felt, to rid myself of the guilt was to confess to Adam, which I was sure wouldn't go well.

"Maybe I'll just hold off telling him for now," I reconsidered. If things were finally good between us again, I didn't want to ruin it.

"Mommy, are we almost home?" My daughter asked with words that held more symbolism than she could ever know.

"Yes, baby, we're almost home." The flight had been long and the time away from my husband brutal but, finally, we crossed over the Pacific to our own personal heaven.

"Thank God," Andrew rejoiced. "I'm so happy to be home."

"Me too, buddy," I replied. "Me too."

The three of us walked off of the plane to see Adam standing, anxiously, in anticipation. He held a handful of white orchids and gifts for our children.

"Daddy!" Anabel exclaimed with a leap into his arms, joined by our son. I smiled at the vision of my husband knelt down with our children in his embrace. I couldn't wait for my turn.

"Hi, beautiful," he greeted with a look of adoration in his eyes. Adam was so handsome with his addictive smile and spellbinding eyes.

He held me, tightly, to his chest, his cologne intoxicating me, as it always did. Each of us refused to let go of our embrace as tears threatened my eyes.

"I've missed you, so much, baby doll," he said, running his fingers through my hair. I had so missed the nickname he'd dubbed me years ago.

"I've missed you, too," I concurred. "It's nice to be home."

"I've missed the ocean," Andrew commented. "I'm just meant to be a beach bum."

"Me, too," his sister agreed.

"Uh oh," Adam replied as we laughed.

Hawaii had welcomed me back, so lovingly, like only it could with its soothing tropical air and aqua waters. I couldn't wait to get back to my house, surrounded by my own things. Our home and family meant everything to me.

"Oh, it's so great to be home," I said, opening the door to my idyllic world. "Wow, and you kept it clean!" I joked.

"Hey, one thing the military has taught me is that filth is not an option," Adam replied. "I know how to clean."

"Yeah, he does a fine job," Andrew added, evoking my giggle.

"In all seriousness, there were a few days there that I was afraid you weren't coming back."

"Me too." I thought back to the day I'd left, the rain pouring down and my future so uncertain, and I never wanted that feeling back.

"I'm so sorry, babe," Adam said with my hands in his, "for how I acted, the hurt that I caused. The alcohol and what happened in Iraq, it all just really messed me up, but you leaving woke me up. I got the help that I needed and still am. I'm only taking my new medication, and I'm still doing PTSD counseling."

"It was bad," I agreed. "You were definitely not yourself, at times, but I'm glad you're getting help. Being away taught me a lot, mostly that I love you and this family more than anything, and I never want to lose it."

"Me either, babe," he replied. "That was the worst feeling I've ever experienced. I can't live without you and the kids." My husband pulled me close to him, holding me securely, and his embrace protected me. It was the only place I wanted to be.

"While you settle in, I've got some apologizing to do with my son and daughter," Adam said in a retreat to their rooms.

It felt wonderful to be home again, and I hoped that our lives could all go back to normal. I still wasn't sure what the future held, but the moment lent a feeling of life being good again.

"Thank you," I prayed with my eyes to Heaven.

I unpacked our suitcases before heading to the back deck to soak up the view that I had missed so much. Hawaii was an entirely different land from the rest of the world. Everything seemed more vibrant, more alive to me. It breathed life back into me.

The hands of my husband fell, gently, onto my shoulders from behind me, and he kissed me on the neck.

"I never asked how your trip was," he said.

"Well, parts of it were really good," I told him. "I visited my parents, your parents and even got to hang out with Mark and Andrea."

"Oh yeah? Great! How are they?" Adam and I sat down, together, for the conversation.

"They're good. We met some old high school friends out for a couple of drinks." I didn't dare mention Casey.

"That's great, babe," Adam replied. I'm glad you had a good time."

"Yeah, but other parts of the trip were misery. I missed home. I missed you and, inside, I was just dying. This is my home and this where I belong, here with you and our children."

Part of me was tempted to confess to my husband what had happened with Casey. The last thing I wanted was to hurt Adam but the guilt was consuming me. I didn't want there to be any secrets between us. The other part of me disputed the confession, knowing how much it would hurt him. Our marriage was finally in a good place again, and I didn't want to ruin it.

"I've got a lot of making up to do," Adam admitted, "so I'm glad you came back to give me the chance." Our conversation was interrupted by the doorbell.

"There's my girl!" Delilah greeted when I opened the front door, and she hugged me tightly. "Welcome home." We were like sisters who hadn't seen each other in years, hugging, giggling and talking nonstop. "I missed you, my friend," she told me. "I had no one to talk to while you were away."

"I missed you, too, and it's so nice to be back home," I replied. "Colorado is nice but Hawaii is home."

"How are things with you and Adam?"

"Really great, so far, but time will tell, I guess."

Delilah and I talked about my trip and, even as much as I trusted her, I couldn't bring myself to mention Casey and what had happened. Still, I wanted to. I needed someone to confide in about my affair, and I needed advice about whether to tell my husband about it.

Casey frequented my mind, even as much as I didn't want him there. I still thought about our time together, the way that he'd made love to me, how much I enjoyed it. His words replayed themselves in my mind.

"You're the one who got away. It should be me in his shoes." They weren't easily forgotten. My heart was elated that he still had love for me, and his words inflated my ego. Even still, I had chosen my husband over Casey, so why did he continue to invade my mind?

On my first night back home, I climbed into my bed, beside my husband. It felt wonderful to be back in his arms, where I was secure and happy.

"This is so nice," Adam commented. "I love you, so much, Allison." He gently caressed my forehead, the way that he often did.

"I love you, too, babe," I responded, and I truly meant my words. He was my heart and soul.

Adam kissed me, slowly and passionately, my entire body being blissfully ignited in fervor. His caress evoked goose bumps on my skin as his fingers traced my silhouette.

"I missed you so much," he whispered. "I missed this."

I hadn't allowed my husband's touch since I'd found out about his affair. I had missed it and I craved it. I was no longer fearful, and I wondered if that was because my own infidelity had somehow validated me.

Adam was careful with his intentions, afraid of being halted again, but I was completely willing. In some strange way, Casey had caused me to want Adam even more, and I was ready to make love to him again.

His lips trekked, slowly, to my neck and, gradually, to my breasts and stomach as the rest of my body hungered for him. He emitted a soft moan as I ran my fingers through his short hair and urged him further downward, where he took his time pleasing me, teasing and caressing me, gently, to gratification. I guided him back up to return the favor.

"Oh, you're amazing," he complimented breathlessly.

A few minutes was all that he could take before lifting me onto him with a slow gyration of his hips, and he pulled my lips down to his. He kissed me, hungrily, passionately, as our bodies danced together in erotic harmony until, together, we quaked, uncontrollably, in blissful delight.

"Wow, that was incredible!" Adam agreed with a grin.

"It's been so long."

"I know. I'm sorry," I told him.

"It was well worth the wait," he replied, caressing my cheek. "I love you more than anything in the world, Allison. You're my heartbeat, my breath." He gazed into my eyes and returned his velvet lips to mine.

"I love you, too," I told him.

"Please say that you forgive me," he whispered.

Remorse flooded me as I lay with my husband, the man I loved, our intimate moment tainted by my infidelity. As much as I fought to block it, I knew that I deserved what I felt. I forgave him but could he forgive me? In so many ways, what I had done was worse than his indiscretion.

The next morning, Adam went off to work, and the kids and I had breakfast before heading down to the beach.

"Stay in the shallow water," I reminded my young swimmers.

I lay back on the oversized blanket, gleefully encompassed by the sun that never failed to soothe me. It was fantastic to lay back and relax with my thoughts, and I was so appreciative to be back home. The ring of my cell phone invaded my euphoria.

"Hi, honey", I answered, assuming that it was my husband on the other end.

"Well then, hello," the deep, all too familiar voice greeted.

"Casey?"

"How are you?" He asked.

"I'm fine... fine," I stammered, surprised by his call.

"Are you back to the tropical beaches and hula skirts?"

"Uh, yes, I'm actually on the beach right now." I wanted to end the small talk. "What's going on?"

"Nothing," he casually responded. "Just wanted to make sure you got home safely."

"Oh, well, thanks."

"I've been really thinking a lot about you since you left," he said.

"Okay, see, you can't do that, Casey. I'm back home with my family." I was perturbed by his gesture and preferred to have no contact with him. "How did you even get my number?"

"Your brother," he replied. "Listen, I don't mean any harm, here, Allison, and I'm sorry if I bothered you. I just had you on my mind and wanted to hear that you got home alright. That's all." I was skeptical but willing to give him the benefit of the doubt.

After checking on Andrew and Anabel, I resumed my position on the blanket where my thoughts took over. I couldn't stop myself from imagining my life with Casey, living in his house together, with my children. I envisioned a completely different life of working, dinners with my parents and outings with Mark and our old friends, to football games at our former high school or nights at the little neighborhood bar. I thought about what marriage to Casey would be with all of the chemistry between us, and I imagined long, passionate nights together. I'm ashamed to admit that I saw happiness and contentment. It was a life that included a man who was there full-time rather than a servant to the military but it was selfish. My husband was a hero that Casey couldn't even begin to compare to. I didn't fight as hard as I should have to push my old flame out of my mind. It gave me something other than my husband's affair to think about, something private for myself that even left me with a bit of a thrill.

"Mom!" The beckoning of my son's voice interrupted my fantasy. "Mom, watch me ride this wave," he called out from his body board, and I observed as a set of small waves shoved him toward the sand on his stomach.

"Whoa, awesome!" I complimented.

"I can do it, too," Anabel competed, riding in the next set.

"You guys are amazing!" I told them.

"Try it, Mom," Andrew urged and, with some hesitation, I made my way into the water.

"Where's my beautiful family?" I heard Adam say when he arrived home from work, later that afternoon.

"Hi, honey," I greeted him with a kiss.

"Mmm, that was nice," he responded with a flirtatious grin. "Give me another one." He pulled me, tightly, to him.

"Oh, not again!" Our son remarked with displeasure at the sight of our affection, and Adam and I laughed as he tapped me on the butt.

"What did you guys do today while your poor ol' dad practiced his drills?" Adam asked Andrew.

"We did some body boarding."

"A beach day while I was stuck out in the heat?" Adam teased. He grabbed his son, tickling him, and Andrew's laughter provoked mine. Anabel ran into the living room where Adam did the same, evoking her endless giggles. I smiled at the three of them and how truly blessed we were. On the couch, our children sat in the arms of their father, contently watching television while I started dinner.

CHAPTER 15

The week that followed was joyous for our family. For the first time in months, everything appeared to be normal again, and I was enormously relieved and looking forward to the future. Adam continued his counseling without any more episodes, seemingly coping more normally in the civilian world. Our family had finally found peace again.

I sat outside in the morning, enjoying a cup of coffee before starting my errands, when the phone rang. The caller's number came up unknown.

"Hello?"

"Hey gorgeous," Casey greeted and my heart raced. "How are you?"

"I'm fine, Casey, and you?" I struggled to disguise my agitation.

"Better now," he said. "I know I'm not supposed to be calling anymore, but I just needed to hear your voice. I don't know what it is, but I'm missing you like crazy. Are you feeling that at all?"

"Sometimes," I wanted to say but didn't because I didn't want our single night together to be misconstrued into something more than it was. I did still think of Casey but I had chosen my husband. "No," I answered his question. "Whatever we had was only that night and it's over now. I want to be with my husband. You can't keep calling me, Casey."

"I know. I'm sorry. I guess I'm just feeling a lot of strange emotions but, the thing is, that night, it brought back so many feelings for me. I lost you once and now, it's like I just don't want to lose you again. But you weren't even mine anyway, right?" Casey rambled on as if his mind and, perhaps, his heart were cluttered with uncertainty. Maybe mine was too. I knew that absence could disregard the feelings, both his and mine, but not as long as we were still talking. I needed to push him back out of my life.

"Casey, please, no more phone calls. This is my life and where I want to be, so that's it, okay?"

"Can't we at least remain friends?"

"No, it's done!" I hung up the phone. I was afraid of him damaging my already fragile marriage, and I was also afraid of my own feelings.

Things were going great between Adam and me since the kids and I had returned from Colorado. Our relationship was finally healing. We were happy again, reverted back to the giddiness that we'd felt when our relationship first began. We were falling in love all over again, and it was euphoria. Even our children seemed more content. We had gained back our happy home. I have to admit that I had nearly even forgotten about Adam's affair with Ezra. Maybe my own had somehow been responsible but, whatever the reason, I no longer held on to the feelings of jealousy and betrayal, and letting go of them granted me precious freedom.

My situation with Casey, however, continued. He'd limited his unwanted phone calls to text messages.

I'm still n luv w/ u, one read, and my demands for him to stop was to no avail. *I want 2 c u again*, another read.

Absolutely not! I responded, but it seemed like my insistence for him to stop only fed his determination and, somewhere in his mind was the belief that I might actually leave Adam for him if he was persistent enough.

I luv it when u play hard 2 get, he'd say.

I was always sure to delete Casey's messages, like a child concealing information she didn't want her parents to see, and I felt terrible for the secrets I kept from my husband, but I didn't want any issues in our remedial marriage.

"Hi gorgeous," he greeted me with a kiss.

"How was your day, babe?"

"Not bad. How was yours?" I mentioned the kids' school orientation, being held that evening. "It's at six so I thought I'd just pick up something for dinner on the way home."

"I'll go with you," he offered.

"You don't have to do that, honey. You worked all day so you stay and relax," I said.

"It's alright. I want to go and meet their teachers."

"Can we stop for ice cream afterward?" Anabel queried in her sweetest voice.

"We haven't had dinner yet," I reminded her.

"I'll try to talk her into it," Adam added with a wink at our daughter.

"You need to stop being a pushover, Daddy," I ribbed about how he could never tell her no.

"She knows her daddy never lets her down," he grinned. "I could make it up to you," he whispered seductively from behind me with his hands around my waist.

"Oh, you could, huh? Well, I'll take you up on that later." My stomach fluttered with delight.

"Well, in the meantime, turn around here and give this lovestruck man a kiss." I turned to receive his satin lips, softly relishing mine in a kiss that beamed of devotion, proving his love for me, and I melted into his arms. My cell phone chimed with a text message, selfishly marring our beautiful moment.

Wish u were mine, the message from Casey said, almost as if he could see me with Adam. I deleted it without responding, then, *Can't help thinking of u.*

"Who's that, babe?" Adam casually asked while getting a drink from the refrigerator.

"Just Andrea," I fibbed. "She's talking about Mark's birthday next week." My heart raced from the blatant lie I had told my husband.

"Speaking of birthdays, did Anabel decide what she wants to do for hers next month?"

"Actually, she has," I replied. "We'll be doing a party and sleepover for the princess and her court."

"Ah," he ribbed, "there shall be makeovers and late-night gossip."

"Precisely, my king," I giggled.

"Are we ready to go?" Our eager son, finely clad in new school clothes and shoes, queried. Adam and I were surprised to see his hair gelled and combed, given his usual unconcerned look.

"No, son, we still have a half hour. What's the rush?"

"Mother, I don't want to be the last one there."

"You won't be, and stop calling me 'mother'."

"Are you wearing cologne?" Adam probed.

"I dabbed a little on," he replied coyly.

"Smells like you bathed in it," his father teased.

"You can never smell too fresh, Dad." Their conversation made me laugh.

"Well, you've got a point there, son," Adam replied with a grin. Shaking my head in amusement, I retreated to Anabel's room to fix her hair.

"You smell bad," she told her brother in the car.

"No, sweetheart, he can never be too fresh," Adam joked.

"He wants to smell good for Emily," she blurted.

"Do not!" Andrew rebutted.

"Ah, yes, a man walks through fire to impress a beautiful lady," Adam said. "I went to great lengths to win over your mom."

"Like what?" Our curious son inquired.

"Well, I bought her flowers and always made sure to tell her how beautiful she is, things to make her smile because it melts my heart." I smiled at my husband with flattery. "If you like Emily, or another young lady, the best thing you can do is make her smile."

"Well said, honey," I spoke with admiration.

I turned my cell phone off during the orientation and, when I turned it back on, four text messages appeared, all from Casey, and I flew into a panic. It was getting to be too much, and I feared Adam finding out.

Hope U R having a good night, the first one read and I deleted it. *Thinking of u*, was the next, followed by, *Can't get u out of my head* and *Wishing u were here with me*. I frantically deleted them all, before Adam could see them, as I fumed. Whatever was causing Casey's continuous texts needed to stop. He'd gone way too far. I felt like he was deliberate in his intentions to break up my marriage.

That's enough! I texted back, and I blocked his number. I wanted him to stay out of my life.

"You coming to bed?" Adam asked, later that night.

"Yeah, I'm just going to read my email real quick first." I scanned through a handful of emails and found one from Casey. "Are you kidding me?" I thought, appalled by his disregard for my requests for him to halt contact with me.

My sweet Allison, it read, please accept my apology for whatever I have done to offend you but know, also, that I won't apologize for how I feel. Our night together ignited something inside of me that I can't even explain. It left me loving and needing you, something I never expected or intended on. I yearn to see you again. I'm in love with you, and I'll do anything. All my love, Casey.

I couldn't believe what I was reading. How could Casey, a known playboy, suddenly be in love after only one night? I had never seen him act that way before. Maybe I should've been flattered but I was, instead, perturbed by his hounding, and my fear of Adam finding out about us was growing. It was clear that Casey wouldn't give up so I decided to confess my infidelity to my husband.

"There's my baby doll," Adam greeted from our bed with that contagious smile but, immediately, he noticed the despondency in my eyes.

"Babe, I have to tell you something," I said as I sat next to him. With my head hung in disgrace, I battled my conscience for the words.

"What is it?" My concerned husband gently lifted my chin, forcing my eyes to his. I took a deep breath, almost unable to speak.

"While I was in Colorado, I…" My breath seemed to disown me as my heart raced. "Something happened that shouldn't have." He peered at me with confusion. "I um…"

"Just say it, babe," he urged, sensing bad news.

"I cheated," I shamefully blurted while erupting into tears.

He stared at me, with uncertainty, as if unsure that he'd heard me correctly while the tears exploded from my eyes.

"I'm so sorry, Adam. I'm so sorry. I didn't mean to hurt you," I said as he sat, frozen and stunned. I needed him to say something, to react, but he couldn't. "I didn't do it to get even."

"Who?" He finally responded in a cracked voice.

"It was Casey," I admitted softly.

"Casey, your old boyfriend?" I nodded slightly, drowned in shame. His face wreaked of disgust and disappointment. "Him, of all people?"

"I didn't go in search of him or anything. He was just there the night that I met up with friends," I explained. "I know I was wrong, Adam. I guess I liked the attention after all that was going on here."

"Don't blame this on me, Allison," he rebutted angrily, and he was right. I had no one to blame but myself. "After all you put me through and then you go and do it. Have you done this before, when I was overseas?"

"No, never!" I exclaimed, needing him to believe me. "I've always been faithful."

"Why him? You have history there. Do you love

him? Do you want to be with him?"

"No, not at all, and it will never happen again, Adam. I promise you. It was the worst mistake of my life." My tearful pleas weren't enough.

"I mean, this is someone you once loved. You were in love with him. This wasn't just sexual," he steamed with disbelief. "I need some time with this," he said and headed for the couch.

"Adam, please, I love you, only you."

"Just give me some time," he replied, calmly but visibly upset. I understood his reaction, having been there, too, so I didn't push the issue. Instead, I lay, alone with my guilt, hoping for his forgiveness.

For two days after my confession, Adam barely spoke to me, even going out of his way to avoid me. It broke my heart to see him hurt and, more so since I was the cause of it. I knew, all too well, how he felt, the agony that he was forced to endure and I wanted desperately to take it away from him. I needed him to forgive me and I hoped, in time, that he would.

His silence was finally broken when he came home from work with anguish in his face, his rigid jaw line tightly clenched.

"I'm going back to Iraq," he announced blankly, with no emotion. My heart sank, the way it always did when I was informed of his tours.

"Already? Why?" I was flabbergasted. He had just gotten home a few months earlier. "How can they send you back after all the problems you had?"

"Actually, I volunteered this time," he replied. "I've been cleared by the therapist so I'm flying out tonight." He spoke casually about returning to war, as if his decision didn't affect anyone. My heart fell to my stomach. It was devastating to me.

"You volunteered?" I echoed. "Is life here, with me, that bad that you'd rather be at war?"

"No," he simply answered.

"Well, then, I don't understand. Is it Ezra?" I remembered her name, vividly, the mistress of my husband. My anger was threatening control of me. "Is it because of what I did?"

"It's not any of that, Allison." Adam hung his head, submitting to his feelings. I kneeled in front of him, taking his hands in mine.

"You don't have to go, Adam. Don't go back there. We can fix all of this. I promise, I'll do anything. Please, just stay with us. The kids and I need you here." I pleaded to the wounded eyes of a tortured soul, knowing that my words were causing him to reconsider, but he didn't.

"I've already committed myself for duty."

"Can't you tell them you've changed your mind?" I was desperate to keep him at home. "What about the kids?"

"They're always in good hands with you," he said. "Listen, we need to take this time apart to save our marriage and decide how much we really need each other. Besides, I'm more beneficial over there than I am here." He had the face of the brave soldier that he was, who performed his duty without involving his emotions.

"How long will you be gone?" Desolation enveloped me at the thought of being separated again.

"I'll be back before Christmas." His words were firm and his tone icy, and it made me want to scream.

"I forgave you, so why can't you forgive me?" I wanted to yell. He was running from the problem, so how could we find a solution? "You selfish bastard!" I wanted to say, but it was I who was selfish.

"I'm a Marine with a job to do," he told me and retreated to our room to pack, emotionless and seemingly uncaring.

With my face in my hands, I cried, weeping for my marriage and my husband. I prayed for strength and understanding as I heard our children cry for him when he told them goodbye. There was no sound worse in the world, and I had no strength of my own. I was enraged at him for leaving them that way because his issue with me wasn't their fault. I held Andrew and Anabel as their father, tearfully, walked out the door.

CHAPTER 16

I awoke with swollen eyes the next morning and peered at the kids in my bed, still asleep. We'd been up together for hours after Adam left, mourning our loss until we had finally cried ourselves to sleep, so I decided to keep them home from school. It had to be so much harder for them, I thought, accepting their father's career, because it meant frequent goodbyes. They didn't quite understand the way that adults did, but they had adapted through the years. As a military family, there was no other choice. It was unfair to them because they hadn't chosen it.

I eased quietly, out of bed, to let them rest, and headed for the bathroom, where I hoped a cold washcloth would reduce the swelling of my eyes. The mirror revealed an image of someone who'd just been to battle. I thought of Adam and where he was, hoping that I'd hear from him soon and, meanwhile, fearing that I wouldn't. It was such a heavy burden on my heart to know that our marriage could be over, and I couldn't bear the thought that we had parted on bad terms. Part of me even shamefully questioned his motive, wondering if my infidelity would drive him back to Ezra again.

"How am I going to get through this?" I asked my image in the mirror. I felt desperate and drained, like I had nothing left in me. How could I help my children cope if I wasn't sure I could cope, myself? My hope was gone.

I started the coffee pot and sat down at the computer, hoping for an email from Adam. What I found was another from Casey.

My sweet Allison, your smile invades my mind, endlessly, taunting my lonely heart. There isn't a woman in the world who can replace you. I dream of holding you in my arms and loving you forever. Trying to forget, Casey.

His words that might have, in better circumstances,

melted my heart nauseated me. I was reminded again of the agony that I'd caused my husband, and I hated myself for it. I hated Casey too, and I wanted nothing more to do with him. He was the obstacle in my marriage. I hoped that ignoring him would convince him to stop contacting me.

Andrew and Anabel woke up in a slightly better mood, though they still grieved their father's absence. After so many years of him coming and going, they had grown accustomed to months at a time without him. It was always hard for them, but they dealt with it amazingly well. I was envious of their resilience, wishing that I had even half of their coping skills. They were my only source of strength. I admired them as they amused themselves with Nickelodeon on the television. The phone rang and I ran to it, hoping to hear Adam's voice.

"I heard he left. How are you holding up?" My loyal friend, Delilah, was always there for me. She was my confidant and the sister I never had. I burst into tears before I could even respond to her. "I'm coming over," she said. We sat outside with our coffee, relishing the sun- kissed breezes.

"This time, it's different," I told her of Adam's departure. "It's my fault."

"You can't blame yourself, Allison."

"We've had our share of problems lately, and he didn't leave on good terms." I had never mentioned Adam's affair, or mine, to Delilah but suddenly, I found myself telling her everything. "I'm so ashamed of what I did," I admitted. "I didn't plan on it, and I didn't do it because he did. I just experienced feelings for Casey that I hadn't felt in years, feelings that I thought were gone. It was like falling in love again. It sounds ridiculous even saying it, but it just felt so right at the time. Now, I know it's the worst thing I've ever done."

Delilah listened to me, without judgment, and said, "You've both made mistakes, but you love each other and you will move past it."

"I really hope so," I said. "Meanwhile, Casey won't stop contacting me, no matter how much I tell him to stop." I told her about his text messages and emails. "I just want him to stay out of my life so I can fix my marriage."

"My advice is to ignore Casey and overwhelm Adam with love. Make him understand that it's him you want," she said. "He probably needs that more than anything right now." She was right, as always. I took Delilah's advice and texted Adam's cell phone.

I love you so much & I'm missing u, I typed.

Hours later, when I still hadn't heard back from him, I convinced myself that he was just too busy to respond, but I wasn't sure of that being the case. I thought of him constantly, wishing that he would somehow walk through the door. I must have checked my cell phone every fifteen minutes for a message from him. That night, I dialed his number and got his voicemail.

"Hi. It's me," I said. "I'm not even sure what to say other than that I can't get you off my mind and that the kids and I miss you so much. You really are my life, Adam, and I love you more than anything. I just really need you," I spoke. "Please call me when you can to let me know you're okay." The tears of my anguish flowed from my eyes as I nursed my broken heart. I needed to hear my husband's voice. Once again, I cried myself to sleep.

The next morning, I dragged myself out of bed, and it was all that I could do. My anguish refused to allow me to face the world. It tempted me to bathe in my self- pity, beneath my covers, and drown in my tears. I heard Delilah's voice on the answering machine, inviting me out for breakfast, but I couldn't convince myself to see anyone. I was trapped in my despair without the will to free myself. My marriage had met its end, I felt, no matter how desperate I was to save it.

My mind refused any thought that wasn't Adam. I

wondered how he was and what he was doing and, most of all, I wondered what he was feeling. I wished that I could hear his thoughts. Was he still willing to fight for our marriage or would he just walk away? I couldn't bear the notion of life without him, and I was willing to do whatever it took to make our marriage succeed. We had both made mistakes but I wanted, desperately, to move past them and repair the wounds that they'd left behind.

Before I knew it, Delilah was knocking on the front door.

"Allison, honey, are you okay?" I heard her call to me, but I didn't want to answer the door. I needed to be alone with my thoughts. "I know you're in there," she said, but I still didn't respond and I felt guilty for my rudeness. "Okay, I understand," she finally added as if able to read my mind. "Just call if you need me." I appreciated her understanding.

The next several hours of my day were spent sulking in a river of tears. I was questioning my own integrity and even questioning God as if it wasn't ourselves who had endangered the perfect marriage that he had created. No matter how much I prayed, Adam didn't respond to me, and it was killing me inside.

Somehow, I managed to pull myself together and pick up the kids from school, performing my best rendition of "nothing is wrong with mom", and I resumed my duties of cooking and cleaning up that evening. If either of them saw through my façade, they didn't mention it.

That night, I tried calling Adam again but was forced into his voicemail.

"I'm thinking of you constantly and praying that you're okay. I just really need to hear your voice, Adam. I miss you so much. Please, call me. I love you so very much." I nearly had to force myself to hang up the phone, somehow believing that he would answer. I lay in bed alone, dreaming of the man I loved and hoping that he was dreaming of me, too.

The next two days without a response from Adam rendered me a robot, functional in my daily routine but numb to its effects. I was treading through the hours in a haze. My anguish was evolving into irritation over his neglect.

"The least he could do is call his children," I thought, irked by his selfishness. I understood that I had betrayed him, terribly, but he'd done the same to me. I had forgiven him but he couldn't do the same, and our mistakes were not the fault of our children. "Hypocrite!" I told myself then that if he didn't care enough to work on our marriage, then I needed to pick myself up and carry on without him. It was time to stop wallowing in guilt and self-pity. Our children still depended on me to be strong for them. "I'm done feeling sorry for myself," I told Delilah when I called her.

"Well, I'm glad to hear it. I was worried about you. Have you heard from him?"

"Not once since he left. He won't return my calls and texts," I replied. "Maybe it's over. I mean, he doesn't seem committed to trying. Maybe it's her."

"Who?"

"Ezra, the woman he had an affair with," I said. "I mean, he did volunteer to go back there."

"As hard as it is, you have to focus on yourself and the kids and not worry about what he's doing," my friend advised. She was right, and my children were my main focus, but Adam was my husband, a priority that I couldn't just let go of.

As much as I fought it, Ezra had found a home in my mind. I couldn't block the image of her with my husband. The thought of them together, intimately embraced, had seared itself in my eyes, burning them in torturous jealousy, and I wondered if I'd lost him to her. Maybe Adam loved her but hadn't had the courage to admit it. Maybe he'd gone back to assess his feelings for her and, worse, maybe it was I who drove him there. Perhaps I was the deciding factor. Even as committed a soldier as he was, I couldn't fathom another reason for him wanting to return to war in such a fragile stage of our marriage.

Nearly a week had passed without a word from my husband, and I was worried. We had never gone that long without contact during any of his tours which, to me, meant that he was either really furious or had been injured in Iraq. I almost expected the military officers to show up at my door because he would have kept in touch with our children, no matter what the circumstances between him and me were. I knew in my heart, that something wasn't right.

CHAPTER 17

My heart sank when I saw two of Adam's friends, and fellow officers, standing at my front door. Clad in their uniforms and somber faces, I battled to hold myself up, certain that they had come with news that Adam was injured or even dead.

"Good afternoon, Allison," one spoke as they respectfully removed their hats.

"What happened? Is he okay?" I probed in a frantic struggle to catch my breath. My pounding heart reverberated throughout my entire body. I knew Joe and Sammy well, having been friends with them and their wives for years and spending many occasions together.

"May we come in?" We all sat down as I braced myself for the worst. "He's okay," Joe began and I breathed a sigh of relief.

"Thank God," I replied. "What happened?" The men flashed each other a quick glance.

"Adam is in some trouble and has been detained in Iraq," Sammy informed me.

"Trouble? What kind of trouble?" I asked. "Stop beating around the bush and make your point." I was growing nervous and agitated by their hesitation. "Come on, guys, level with me."

"He's been held for killing an Iraqi woman, intentionally. He shot her at point blank range." I felt like their news had stopped my own heart, as well.

"What? He killed a woman there?" I needed to hear their words again for them to be real. "This has to be a mistake. Both of you know Adam. He would never do something like that." I was dumbfounded and in disbelief, unable to grasp the truth of what I had just heard. A thousand questions entered my mind. Who was the woman? Why would he do such a callous thing? It all felt like a nightmare that I couldn't escape. "How could he take someone's life without being forced to?" I asked myself. It wasn't, at all, in his character.

"We don't know yet," Sammy responded grimly. "He's been detained, and they are doing an investigation right now."

"This just doesn't make any sense," I said. "Can I talk to him?" I needed to tell Adam that I was there for him and that it was clearly a misunderstanding that would work itself out.

"I'm afraid you can't right now, Allison. I'm sorry."

"If there's anything that we can do…" Joe offered.

"Thanks. I appreciate that," I replied, walking them to the door. My head was spinning with questions. "How could this have happened?" I asked myself. "What would I tell our children?" It was clear that Adam wouldn't be coming back home anytime soon and I was angry at him for leaving us, alone, to pick up the pieces. I wondered how he could take the life of a woman and why. I felt that it had to have been an accident or some kind of misunderstanding, and the despair of not knowing what was going on was too much to bear. I needed answers.

I wanted to crawl into a deep hole, where I didn't have to face anyone or deal with what had happened. Instead, I was forced to wear a courageous face for our children. It wouldn't do them any good to lose both parents.

"Honey, are you alright?" Delilah probed when she brought Andrew and Anabel home from the beach, later that day.

"Is it that obvious?" I replied. My eyes must have revealed my sad story.

"Kids, go play," she instructed her and my children to lend us some privacy. I confided in my friend about my visit from Joe and Sammy, that morning, and what they had told me about my husband. It felt strange to even be repeating their words.

"I can't believe it," I said. "I don't know what to

do." Her expression told of surprise and dismay, though she remained calm and collected.

"There must be a misunderstanding," she said.

"That's what I thought, too, but they said there isn't," I replied.

"You know that I'm here for you. Steve and I, both, are for whatever you need. We're going to get through this. I promise."

"Well, I guess all I can do, right now, is wait," I said. There was nothing that anyone could do to help me, and I knew that the wait would be brutal. I knew that it could be months, even years, until I saw my husband again, and the thought of that was agonizing. Still, I was forced to go on with my life.

It was days later when I opened the mailbox and found a letter from Adam. My heart must have skipped a thousand beats at the mere sight of his handwriting. I held the envelope tightly in my trembling hands, anxious for his words but terrified, all at the same time. At the small, round kitchen table, I stared at the envelope, my future in its hands.

"Open it," I urged myself, several times over, until finally, I did. My quivering fingers fumbled longer than they should have.

My Babydoll, life is always a game of chance that only a lucky few can win. Decisions alter the future, and the wrong ones are often catastrophic. So many times, they can't be repaired, and maybe that's what happened to us. My affair was the biggest mistake of my life because it destroyed you, and I never, ever wanted to hurt you. I was supposed to protect you, protect your heart, but I failed. My affair caused yours, and it broke me to know that you were with another man, even if I did deserve it. Inside, I couldn't stop screaming but, worst of all is the realization that I caused it with my bad decision. It gnaws at my gut that I ran you into his arms, that maybe he gave you something that I couldn't. All I want to do is heal the pain that I've caused but there's only one way to do that. I'm removing the demons and hoping that you can live again, without your burdens and without your grief. You and our children are my everything, and remembering me in happier times is far easier than coping with what the war has cursed me with. I love you, Allison, with every single fiber of my soul. Tell everyone how sorry I am for Ezra and myself, and tell them I did it out of my endless love for you. I'll always be with you, my sweetheart, my kiss in the gentle breezes. Forever your angel, Adam.

My hands trembled and my body quaked as I battled for breath. Panic consumed me and I could no longer see through my tears as my heart screamed.

"No!" His words had depleted my soul until only the shell of me was left on the floor, a wounded child. My loss was consuming every ounce of my strength, a nightmare that I could never escape. I would be plagued a widow, grudgingly propelled through life without my better half, forced to survive without my soul mate. My tears poured out my desolation. How would I live without Adam, I wondered. How would our children live without their father? It wasn't fair to us, and I was furious at him for taking the easy way out while we were forced to stay behind to suffer in our mourning.

I had to somehow muster the strength for the kids. I was all that they had left, and they would depend on me to help them through our loss. I tried, desperately, to pull myself together before they emerged from the backyard. It was then that I saw Joe and Sammy reappear at the front door. They had come to break the news that I had just found out, and their faces displayed torment of their own as they hugged me. I could see their eyes fill as they read his final words to me in the letter that I showed them.

"I'm so sorry, Allison," Sammy consoled.

"Me, too, and if there's anything that we can do..."

Joe offered. He handed me the silver ID tags that my husband had worn, and I clutched them, tightly, to get a feeling of him.

"Bring him home for a proper burial," I tearfully requested.

"Of course," they assured before they left. After several minutes of trying to gather my strength, I called Andrew and Anabel inside.

"What's wrong, Mommy?" My daughter probed. I kneeled before them, as they sat on the couch, with their hands in mine.

"Daddy... um... he..." I struggled to find the most sensitive words but there were none that would make my news any easier for them. I knew that I was experiencing the worst moment of my life. Nothing had ever been more agonizing. I noticed the fear in their eyes, as if they already knew. "He went home to God."

"No!" Andrew erupted into tears.

"He died?" His sister followed suit, and I held both of them tightly. All I wanted was to protect them from the pain that I was feeling.

"I'm so sorry," I consoled. The three of us wailed, grieving the man who was so special to us. Their agony was mine, and I prayed for God to give their pain to me.

"He was shot?" Andrew asked. In a sense, I would have rather them thought that. Perhaps it would lend more respect for their father than what had really happened to him, but they needed the truth.

"No, honey, but he was very sick. The war, sometimes, affects people in ways that they can't recover from, and that's what happened to Daddy. It's not the military's fault, and it's not ours. He just wanted to be with God, and he's so happy there," I explained. "He loved both of you more than anything else in the world and, although it doesn't seem fair, we're going to be okay." If only I could have bribed my heart to agree with my words.

We were a military family, preened to prepare for the loss of our Marine. Death had always lived in our minds as a possibility of war, yet no amount of preparedness could have eased our pain. I suffered for my children, destroyed by the anguish they felt. It didn't seem fair for them to have to endure such agony, and all I could do was be there for them. Together, we grieved for the man that we loved, the man who took care of us and devoted himself to us. We had always adored and respected Adam as the head of our family, and I didn't know how we would survive without his love and humor. His death devastated us and would change our lives forever. The loss of my husband asphyxiated me and left me convinced that I would never get through the heartbreak that I felt. I wondered how he could end someone's life and end his own. I wondered if he was truly free, in Heaven. Thinking of him there made his death a little easier to cope with.

I thought about Ezra and what she must have felt in her final moments. Perhaps Adam felt that he was, somehow, freeing her, too, reuniting her with her son. Maybe, in his mind, he felt that he was helping us all.

Never had I felt such misery. His absence was permanent. Adam and I had been together for so many years, and he was my soul mate. I wondered how he could leave us to suffer such a loss, but his letter had made it obvious that he felt we were better off without him. I gathered myself and called Adam's parents, dreading the suffering that I would have to bestow on them. I couldn't imagine any worse pain than losing one's child. They didn't know about Ezra or his affair, and I chose not to tell them.

"Is everything okay?" His father probed when he heard my unusually meek and crackling voice. As hard as I resisted, the tears persevered.

"I'm so very sorry to tell you this, Dad, but..." I tried to choke down the lump in my throat. "It's Adam. He's..." I listened to his father's misesry as he mourned the loss of his son, and my heart ached for him. It wasn't news that I wanted to give him over the phone.

"What happened?" He asked after several minutes. I explained how Adam had been affected by the war, though I was vague. I spoke about his nightmares and episodes after his most recent tour.

"The therapy seemed to help after a while," I told him. "No one saw this coming." I didn't reveal to him the inappropriate details of our affairs and his addiction.

After the conversation, I called my own parents, who were also in disbelief. They insisted on flying to Oahu to be with the kids and me, which was a relief because I needed them.

Before I knew it, Delilah and Steve were knocking on the front door.

"Oh, honey, I'm so sorry," she said, hugging me. "We heard the news."

"We're here for whatever you need," Steve consoled with an embrace as Delilah held Andrew and Anabel in her arms, on the couch.

"I guess I'm still kind of in shock," I told them. I was grateful to have them there with us. I wasn't sure how much they knew about what had happened, but I hoped that they were cautious with their words around the kids. I didn't want them to know that their father had taken a woman's life. He needed to remain respectable in their hearts.

I was relieved to see my parents the following day, knowing that they could help out with the kids. I needed the additional support.

"How are you holding up, sweetheart?" My mother asked with a hug at the airport.

"As good as can be expected, I guess," I answered, trying not repeat my habitual crying. "Keeping busy helps. Thanks so much for coming."

"Well, of course we would come, and we're here to

help with whatever you need," she said. "How are the kids dealing with this?"

"They still break down, but they're doing better than I expected. I'm not sure that it has really hit them yet. Of course, I won't tell them what really happened. Adam's parents don't even know. I just don't want to make things worse on them."

"It's better that way, at least for now," my father agreed.

The military was preparing to fly my husband's body home from Iraq, and I was arranging for him to be flown to Colorado, where he could be laid to rest near his family. It seemed surreal to be making funeral arrangements for him, even though the possibility had always been there. I could never have prepared myself enough for the loss of him. I worried about our children, enduring the same loss and being forced to leave their home in Hawaii, where they had grown up. I thought about getting a house off base, in Oahu, so that Andrew and Anabel could remain with their friends for the school year, but they preferred to relocate and be closer to our family. I knew that it would be easy for them to make new friends in Colorado, and they had always loved visiting there. Maybe we all needed the change of scenery.

"All packed?" Delilah asked as we stood in front of the empty house that had created so many of our wonderful memories. Leaving it all behind was excruciating. A part of Adam was there, and a part of us remained there with him. I took a final glance at the house, wondering if anywhere else would feel like home. My throat throbbed with pain as I fought back my tears.

"I think I'm ready," I answered my friend with the fib.

"I'm really going to miss you around here," Delilah said in our farewell hug.

"I'll miss you, too, and I'll come back and visit."

"Steve and I will see you in Colorado for the funeral."

"Thanks, Delilah, for everything," I told her. "I love you."

The children and I left Hawaii with our suitcases full of clothes, for Colorado, where we'd already shipped the rest of our belongings. I stared down at the ocean below us, trying to cope with all that our family had lost. I recalled my last flight, when I had left Adam, and how I felt the same misery that was, again, so familiar to me only, this time, it was permanent. Just like before, I found myself unsure of my future, or even the next step, and it was terrifying to think of starting over. Already, I missed Adam, so much, and the pain was almost more than I could bear. I would have given anything to bring him back. I peered over at my sleeping children, their swollen eyes still red from their tears. They were my survival, my strength and my courage to continue on with life, and I promised them my all that day.

Adam had a military funeral, filled with love and remembrance from those who adored him. Our children and I sat in the front row, along with Adam's parents and mine, all consoling one another. I could feel his spirit in the room, his laughter and his love, soothing us and letting us know that he was happy and finally free.

His funeral was a year ago, and we all still take life day by day, some with grief and others with hope, but always with our heroic Marine in our hearts. We recently bought a house of our own, in Colorado, the kids and me and, though we no longer have the palm trees and shimmering teal ocean, we have our family and a loving home of brand new memories to be made. Adam still shares our home through a wall of photos of him. I still haven't confessed the real story surrounding Adam's death to his parents or to our children. Perhaps it is better to leave them with the dignity of the son they raised.

Today, on the anniversary of his death, we celebrated his life, the joy and love that he graced us with. We recalled his silly antics and laughter, his voice and his heart. When the Autumn sun's warmth yielded a soft breeze, only briefly, I smiled and breathed him in.

"I'll always be with you, my sweetheart, my kiss in the gentle breezes." His words were my strength, his presence, and forever, they live in my soul.

www.ingramcontent.com/pod-product-compliance
Lightning Source LLC
Chambersburg PA
CBHW052135170626
46812CB00004B/1438